CW01212974

GIRL IN A PINK DRESS

KYLIE NEEDHAM

GIRL
IN
A
PINK
DRESS

HAMISH HAMILTON
an imprint of
PENGUIN BOOKS

HAMISH HAMILTON

UK | USA | Canada | Ireland | Australia
India | New Zealand | South Africa | China

Hamish Hamilton is part of the Penguin Random House group of companies whose addresses can be found at global.penguinrandomhouse.com

Penguin
Random House
Australia

First published by Hamish Hamilton in 2023

Copyright © Kylie Needham 2023

The moral right of the author has been asserted.

All rights reserved. No part of this publication may be reproduced, published, performed in public or communicated to the public in any form or by any means without prior written permission from Penguin Random House Australia Pty Ltd or its authorised licensees.

This is a work of fiction. All central characters are fictional, and any resemblance to actual persons is entirely coincidental. In order to provide the story with a context, some real names of places and historical figures are used.

Cover painting (*Untitled S 26*) by Michal Lukasiewicz
Cover design by Sandy Cull
Typeset in Adobe Caslon Pro by Midland Typesetters, Australia

Printed and bound in Australia by Griffin Press, an accredited ISO AS/NZS 14001 Environmental Management Systems printer

A catalogue record for this book is available from the National Library of Australia

ISBN 978 1 76104 696 4

penguin.com.au

MIX
Paper | Supporting responsible forestry
FSC® C018684

We at Penguin Random House Australia acknowledge that Aboriginal and Torres Strait Islander peoples are the Traditional Custodians and the first storytellers of the lands on which we live and work. We honour Aboriginal and Torres Strait Islander peoples' continuous connection to Country, waters, skies and communities. We celebrate Aboriginal and Torres Strait Islander stories, traditions and living cultures; and we pay our respects to Elders past and present.

For Joe and Liv
And for Ben

When one colour approaches slightly to another, it is said to incline towards it; when it stands in the middle between two colours, it is said to be intermediate; when, on the contrary, it evidently approaches very near to one of the colours, it is said to fall, or pass, into it.

Patrick Syme
Werner's Nomenclature of Colours

This is what it is the business of the artist to do. Art is theft, art is armed robbery, art is not pleasing your mother.

Janet Malcolm
The Silent Woman

PROLOGUE

Untitled figure study, ink wash on paper, 77 × 57 cm

She is Eva, under the water, I think.

Halfway through the exhibition, a pair of old men in grey suits and glasses stand dwarfed by a two and a half by two metre painting on a state gallery wall. The painting is of a young woman in a pink dress against a cavernous background of bruised blues and bulky blacks.

She looks mournful. She wears pale flat shoes that are too small for her long feet. The fitted waist, the gathered bust, the dainty pink and red shoulder ties. Sophia Loren in a fifties Italian movie, or at least a pale Australian relative. A lump of darkness looms behind her, around her, above her; a fathomless shape built up in wide horizontal strokes and swells of paint that still look wet.

Her dress looks as if it belongs in another picture, too flirty for this one, too floral, the kind of thing you'd wear to a party or on a date. But I know without reading the wall text beside the painting that she is not going anywhere of the kind. Her eyes tell me this too – distant, heavy as two stones, painted in the same palette as the darkness engulfing her.

Was it deliberate, I still wonder after all this time, the way the artist built her from the same substance as the blackness? And why do the blunt lilac lines of her lips and cheeks, the deep plum hollows of her neck, still appear to me like wounds, as fresh as on the day they were painted nearly twenty-five years ago? Was that how the artist wanted her to look? Injured and lost in a ridiculous pink party dress?

Is that what he saw?

It was a mistake, I start to think, to have come today. I should have left the invitation unopened, unanswered, in my drawer. I should have made up an excuse – too busy, too far away, too anything – to have avoided having to stand here on this shining marble floor surrounded by his family and his gallerists and his collectors and his paintings. I look over my shoulder into the next room where there's a wall of works he made in Barcelona, and consider quietly slipping out. But it is too late now to leave. People have seen me and will interpret an early exit badly.

The grey suits whisper.

One of them glances at me, then turns back to his friend and nods. I can't hear what they're saying but I know. They're saying the woman in the painting is me.

ONE

Bald Hill landscape (dawn), oil on canvas, 40 × 50 cm

Six chooks and only two pale eggs in the boxes this morning. And yesterday the same. Something is putting them off laying. A fox maybe. The pests are never far, skulking near the shed in the milky blue dawn, tugging on the chicken wire, sinking their claws into the pulpy mud at the foot of the door.

Or maybe it's the weird turn in the weather. The bitter cold that's not due here for months has come early, like an over-eager newborn, all shivery and translucent-skinned, with no fat on the bone yet to keep itself warm. It's only April but already the mornings arrive blanketed in frost, the barren ground up here on the rocky plateau disguised for a few hours beneath a powdery white deposit that tourists and campers routinely confuse with snow.

I saw a girl write her name in it once. She was staying at the pub with a motorcycle group, before they banned motorcycles and four-wheel drives on the Candle River Track after a section of the narrow dirt road slipped off the mountain in a storm. She had long hair and no shoes on, just a pair of cut-off denim shorts and a too-big leather jacket with silver studs down the arms and coloured badges on the back that must have belonged to one of the men she was riding with.

She annoyed all the roos, who hopped off in a dozen different directions, their grey tails bobbing, a couple of curious joeys peering out from their mothers' pouches with black eyes like tiny beads, as she ran down Panners Avenue. Past the tall rows of naked maples and bare-branched pines. Past the dilapidated buildings half-slumped to the ground like weary old dogs. A stick in one hand and her dark hair flying out, the main street empty and wide before her, white mist shifting about her legs like smoke. Laughing at who knows what, maybe still drunk from the night before. Maybe that's why her bare feet were numb to the cold.

Her name was Eva. Or at least I assumed that was her name, because that's what she wrote there in the frost, each letter carefully etched with the stick into the frozen dew. She wrote it so big I could see it from my front verandah, where I was standing in my pyjamas and grubby sheepskin boots, my arms stacked with kindling to resurrect the fire inside that had dwindled overnight.

It was gone when I came back from the studio in the afternoon, not that I expected to see it still there. I knew any name, even that one, could only last an hour or so, melting imperceptibly till not even the ghost of it remained on the ground.

And it's never been there any other morning. I know because I often glance over when I step out first thing to bring in the wood and collect the eggs. Just in case.

But any other explanation is not worth thinking about.

It's a common enough name.

The loose black and white tiles on the bathroom floor swing like seesaws under my feet as I step out of the iron tub to dry myself. I've been meaning to repair them for so long now, only it's simpler to drop the thought of doing anything about them – gluing them down, replacing the cracked ones, removing the lot and laying a neat new stable floor – as soon as it arrives in my head. The list of broken things here to fix is too long, I wouldn't know where to begin. So I just leave things as they are.

There's a chill creeping beneath the door, which is too short for the doorframe and peeling with blue paint. The rolled-up bath mat I've stuffed in the gap is doing little to help. I grab a towel and quickly rub my wet skin with it, trying to stay warm, but already my arms and thighs and stomach are stippled with goosebumps. I am ghostly white.

I hang the towel on the hook on the back of the door, and step one leg and then the other into a pair of clean underwear. Nothing fancy, I'm done with all that. Just plain black cotton ones I buy in packs of three from the supermarket when I'm down the mountain; I have a dozen pairs the same. As I'm pulling these ones up I spot a tangle of white pubic hairs growing among the brown ones; more than the last time I looked, as though the whiteness is catching. They are thicker and coarser than the brown hairs, more insistent, which unnerves me. They are taking over.

I tell myself not to mind. That this is the way of things.

When I was younger, I always kept a razor and would tirelessly shave my legs, my armpits, my bikini line. I'd pluck the stray hairs from between my eyebrows and wax the pale down above my upper lip. I'd even remove the wisps of hair that grew on the knuckles of my toes, which was excessive, I know – who notices a girl's toes? Still, it seemed important to appear as bare and unblemished as possible – to be seamlessly blank – when my body was so often looked at, appraised, and recorded. When I'd sit for long hours for Clem. Or those few awkward failed attempts I made at sitting for myself in front of a mirror.

I don't bother with any of it now, though. Removing hair from a body no one sees, let alone draws or paints anymore, feels trivial. And pointless. I don't waste my time.

'Can I trim it?' he used to say, his dark hooded eyes gazing up from between my legs, his mouth damp and glistening, barely waiting for me to nod and pass the scissors.

For some reason I think of that now.

I don't know why.

And then I remember last night I dreamed.

Of that first afternoon. With Clem in a pale-yellow shirt, half the buttons left undone. His tanned legs darting up the stone steps to a rambling cottage smelling of jonquils and bathed in rosy afternoon light.

Me, in my cheap sandals, running to keep up. My cheeks red and sweaty from the hours-long drive in the hot car. The hem of my dress licking the backs of my damp legs like a thirsty tongue.

'Frances, come on!' Clem waving from the verandah, pushing open the rickety front door. 'Come on!'

I run and run, my sandals slapping the ground, but in the dream I never catch up.

=

I put the tarnished Italian coffeepot on the stove and listen to the *click-click* as I twist the metal knob that sparks the gas. Then I light it with a match.

It's a temperamental old stove, skinny and small, standing upright on four legs more like a piece of furniture than an appliance, with lettering on its pea-green enamel door that's too faded to be legible. Below the lettering is a picture of a kookaburra that has almost entirely rusted off; only a scrap of wing and the tip of a beak remain. It's also missing a few parts – some bolts, a hinge, one of the heavy cast-iron grates – that Van, the only local electrician, says I'll be lucky to find in a museum.

I should have thrown out the stove long ago. Replaced it with a new one that's reliable and isn't a day-long event to clean. But something about it still appeals to me. Its resilience, perhaps. Its refusal to sputter out and die inelegantly in a tip.

Or maybe it's a memory that holds me back. Of using it here for the first time, the two of us overloading it with bubbling copper pots that hadn't been touched for years. Me, wide-eyed, knowing nothing about cooking, taking direction from Clem about when to stir, when to add herbs, when to taste. The unfamiliar smells of stewing rabbit, star anise, cardamom and thyme warming the cottage, seeping into the walls and floors and ceiling so I could still smell them in the dark when I was falling asleep, my head red-wine-heavy on Clem's chest, my ear pressed to the low drum of his heart, my naked body knotted around his like a vine. His boxes and suitcases, and my brown leather satchel, and our rolls of blank canvas and paints waiting patiently by the door, like Christmas presents, to be unwrapped.

The worn floorboards complain as I walk into the front room, where there's space for a lumpy couch, a lamp, an overstuffed bookshelf and not much more. I stand in front of the open fire and wait for the coffee to brew, holding my hands close to the orange flames to catch a little of their warmth. The cottage smells so smoky and dank after the crisp dawn air outside, as if I've stuck my head inside a smouldering campfire. The rug, the couch, the blue and green plaid blanket covering it like a shroud, the dozens of paintings crowding the walls – some mine, some swaps with other artist friends, a series of framed finger-paintings, an interior by Albert Hughes that he gave me in the late nineties with a note, the paper now yellowed but still neatly tucked at the back, between the stretcher and the canvas: 'Yours to sell, dear Frances, should you ever need' – everything smells thick and stale and black with it.

I pick up one of the cushions that has sunk into a corner of the couch and couldn't look any flatter if I'd driven over it with my ute. I try to plump it up to make the room look more cheerful, less neglected. But as I do, tiny particles of ash spill out – the result of twenty-something years spent opposite an open fire, sucking in its detritus.

I watch the ash as it tumbles in the air, neither falling nor climbing, just swimming in circles in a thin band of sunlight coming through the window. For a moment it seems possible it might stay that way forever, the particles floating and whirling in unison, holding together like a flock of birds in their own unknowable rhythm. But eventually the dust becomes too heavy and softly sinks back into the couch. I leave the rest of the cushions alone, deflated but undisturbed.

It's been weeks now (how many? Three?) since the invite from Clem arrived in a glossy envelope, and still I keep being struck by unasked-for memories of how this room used to look. How vibrant and full of promise it seemed when the two of us first moved in, every corner of it shimmering with warm sunlight, a luminous interior painted in blazing yellows and fiery tangerines. Fresh daffodils and purple irises spilling from glass bottles on the windowsills. Jammy-ripe persimmons and furry-skinned quinces picked straight from the tree and heaped in earthenware bowls. The brawny smells of turpentine and linseed oil thickening the air. Clem's gleaming wet paintings propped against every wall, every door, every wobbly and mismatched chair, leaving drips of coloured paint on the floorboards I would try not to tread in with my bare feet. The treacly voice of Nina Simone floating in through the open front door from Clem's portable CD player on the verandah. *I put a spell on you . . .*

Back then the windows were always open. Clem insisted he never felt the cold. 'It's too hot,' he would constantly say, even when the temperature fell to three or four degrees overnight. In our black wrought-iron bed I would feel his legs grow slick and sweaty next to mine if I'd secretly shut our bedroom window after he'd fallen asleep. He'd mumble and groan and turn away from the heat of my body, searching for the cool at the edge of the mattress, beyond the sheet. I'd tiptoe out of bed, my naked body blue and unearthly in the moonlight, to open the window again before he woke up. Then I'd burrow back under the blankets and fold my shivering limbs into his.

The sunsets were pinker then. Wider. Gauzy bands of rich colour wiped across the sky like blush along a cheek.

I don't remember the floorboards creaking, even when we had sex on them. I don't remember there being any dust.

My cottage stands alone on the crest of a hill on the western edge of town, half a kilometre away from Rina, my nearest neighbour. She could be in her fifties or sixties or even seventies, it's hard to tell; nothing about Rina is certain or exact. Her skin is as tough and speckled as a lizard's but it looks more like sun damage than age to me. I imagine her as a girl who sunbathed topless on the beach for hours, not caring who saw, dousing herself in coconut oil and turning her body over and over like a pig on a spit to make her skin fry faster, browner. She's as copper as an old coin now.

Rina cooks five nights a week at the pub and lives alone in an old miner's cottage like mine. Whenever we spot each other across the belt of yellow grass separating my place from hers, we always wave but rarely say hello. Rina's got a beat-up seventies XB Falcon, blue as a wren, that she sits in for hours at a time but doesn't drive. I've never once heard her start the engine. I have my own theory about why she does it, but it's just a theory; a backstory I've made up that is probably untrue, melodramatic. Maybe Rina just likes sitting in her car.

One night at the pub a few years ago, after she'd charred my steak so black and brittle I could have drawn with it, Rina was drunk enough to tell me she'd spent twenty-six months in Silverwater jail.

'For armed robbery,' she said, something hard and challenging in her raspy voice. She was leaning her bony body against the bar and cradling a schooner of beer to her ripe armpit like a tiny pet. Her clothes, as always, swam on her, and I remember thinking it was entirely possible Rina had at some point raided the wardrobe of a dead woman twice her size.

'Never would've picked it, eh?' she said. 'Harmless old bird like me in the clink!'

She winked at me, the baggy skin around her eyes crinkling like paper, the maples out the window behind her waving their fire-coloured leaves. Then she laughed so hard she snorted, spraying spit onto my cheek; whether she realised or not, I wasn't sure. Either way, I resisted wiping it off, which would have felt rude somehow.

'Not sorry for it, either,' Rina said, rubbing her beaky nose on the mucky sleeve of her shirt. 'Not sorry one fuckin' bit. How 'bout that, eh?'

I knew Rina was baiting me, waiting for shock or even terror to appear on my face. Maybe it was her intention to scare me. Probably that would have amused her, to panic the quiet artist-lady living alone next door; to have me bolting my doors and jumping at noises in the dark. Amusements for Rina were surely few and far between. But when I didn't play along – when instead I nodded and said we'd all done shameful things, terrible things people might never understand – Rina grabbed me by the chin with a rough greasy hand that smelled of raw onions and chip oil, and regarded my face the way a mother might, kind of knowing and sad, narrowing her eyes as if she could see inside me.

I've never told anyone else what Rina said about having been in prison. And I've never brought it up with her again (though I've wanted to) or pushed her for details (did she rob a bank? Mug someone who'd wronged her? Use a knife? A gun? Something nastier like an axe?). I haven't asked in case she regretted saying it or was too drunk to remember. Remembering is not always a helpful thing.

The bumpy white walls of my cottage are made of wattle and daub, which would be notable almost anywhere else, but here in Bald Hill, where objects wear their long histories on their skin, it's as common as rock. This was the way they built things here a century and a half ago, when the town was on the cusp of its gold-rush glory, using wooden strips and straw held together with clay, wet soil, probably even horse shit, anything that would stick.

The grander double-storey buildings made of brick and cement – like the pub, the general store and the fire station on the main street, now with a single fire truck too rotten to stamp out a match, let alone a bushfire – came later, in the wild boom of the 1870s, when nuggets of reef gold too weighty to lift and too wide to wrap your arms around burst from the earth like blood from a cut artery. Back when this tiny town, perched on the shelf of a craggy mountain range, throbbed with ten thousand people. Not that anyone could imagine that now. Fewer than a hundred people call Bald Hill home, me included.

Most of the brick buildings have either collapsed and lie in ruins, or are still making their drowsy descents to the dirt. Their verandah posts lean. Their rusted tin roofs sag. Their picket fences, battered and grey, slant like rows of crooked teeth. And all the gold is long gone, unless you count the worthless dust that still travels in the creeks and amuses the sightseers, or else believe the drunken tales you hear late at night at the pub, of mythical vials of buried treasure beneath the floorboards.

On long weekends and during the school holidays, when the tourist buses nose into town like white whales, their massive wheels caked in red dust from the slow jerky drive up the unsealed mountain road, you can usually hear a tour guide pointing out to passengers, who all stare down as one from behind their tinted windows, the remains of Bald Hill's fleeting, incandescent boom: a knee-high tumble of bricks that was once the bank; a patch of white splintery grass that was once the post office; the main street, Panners Avenue, lined for one mile with exotic century-old European trees, silent and deserted now for longer than anyone can recall.

A ghost town. Or a town for ghosts.

But my cottage still stands, as does Rina's and a few others of similar vintage scattered around town. All with the same small square rooms, low ceilings, bare timber floorboards, add-on bathrooms and toilets outside.

I painted a series of these houses for a show I had in Paddington last year, complete with their limp gardens and flimsy iron gates, their flabby armchairs parked on cracked verandahs, and bent brick chimneys blackened with soot. Each like a weary sentinel rendered in pasty yellows and dirty whites, watching over the abandoned mines, eroded gullies and unpeopled streets.

Nine of the twelve paintings sold on opening night, which wasn't a disaster. The others sat in the stockroom until Christmas Eve, when two more sold to a barrister needing a gift for his wife and hoping to look like he'd thought about it. The last work – a painting of my cottage, unframed, a smaller canvas than the rest, the figuration blurred beneath a vast crepuscular sky – was returned to my studio, where I scraped it back and painted over it with something else.

Over the years, and without direct intention, I've accumulated a modest but dedicated following among the mature, well-off women of Sydney's east: lips and nails painted coral red, diamond rings like boulders slipping sideways on arthritic fingers, voices like gravel that are accustomed to being heard. A couple of them – those women who have had a shrewd eye for the best of my paintings since I first began exhibiting in my early twenties, before I'd won any prizes or had a name – have strong collections of my work and have become something akin to friends. They invite me to their parties. They lend me their beach houses. They try to set me up (despite my reluctance) with their favourite wealthy divorcees. They donate my paintings to state museums and regional galleries they believe ought to have them in their collections. Occasionally they even brave the interminable drive up the mountain to my studio, eager for a first look when I'm close to finishing a show.

Sometimes I want to ask them if they realise that when they buy my work, they are buying pictures of decline. Of a town with a dazzling past but a deteriorating future. Of mountains and valleys forever scavenged and scarred. Of buildings so comatose they'll take another century to fully collapse to the ground. But I never do; it's not a question I ever manage to voice out loud. Probably because I'm afraid that if they knew, they'd stop buying my paintings. Or I suppose it's always possible that in my ruined landscapes they see something I don't.

My long-time art dealer, Tobias, tells me not to question it. They love me, he says. They eat it up! My quaint little life in my kooky town and my soft mysterious paintings that don't compete with their designer sofas. Who cares if they don't understand my work? How many artists could ever claim to have been understood? And as long as enough of these women remain willing to spend five figures here or there on my paintings, I still have a reliable career, where plenty of others have sunk into oblivion.

What Tobias does not say, what he will never say – out of kindness or pity or tact, or a combination of all three – is a truth we both suspect but studiously ignore: that it does not hurt sales that I was once connected to Australian art royalty.

It's been so long now, almost twenty-five years, since I've had anything remotely intimate to do with him, and still it's the first thing anyone ever says or writes about me, on those increasingly rare occasions when critics mention female artists in their forties: that I was once the muse and young lover of acclaimed artist Clem Hughes.

My daughter tells me I'm a line on his Wikipedia page.

And so it hovers beside me like a constant shadow: the fear that my paintings only sell – perhaps have only ever sold – because some of Clem's shine has rubbed off on me.

Tobias named the show *Endurance*, a pompous but fitting title that captured not only the theme of the work, but also how I felt at the Friday-night opening, standing in a white void-like gallery on polished concrete for three hours in my high heels and silk dress, nodding and smiling with a glass of champagne and pretending to remember fancy people's names.

I've never been good at these money-soaked functions, even back when I used to try. So little to do with the paintings on the walls, so driven by the egos promenading the room – all of them desperate for you to know who they are, how well-connected and influential they are, how deeply they care about *the art*. Vapid people. With stale handshakes and patronising words of encouragement and ugly wine-stained teeth, and no clue how to make or be moved by a truly great painting, despite owning fifty. They wallpaper their houses with them.

And that city. With its sticky, steamy air and starless sky, stretching all the way out to the flat suburbs where I grew up. It's not for me; it never really was. And I only breathed clean air into my lungs again after I walked back to my ute, threw away the parking fine that had been tucked under the wiper, pulled off my high heels and started the engine, and drove three hours back up the mountain in the pitch dark to Bald Hill.

The bare light bulb beside my front door glows golden, like a miniature sun, against the swollen grey sky. I'm in my painting clothes: a check flannel shirt, a woollen jumper that's already so tatty and stained I don't have to worry about wrecking it, a pair of jeans that are rarely off me long enough to put through the wash, and my paint-encrusted leather boots that need to be replaced next time I'm down the mountain; the stitching is coming undone. Before I close the cottage door behind me, I pull on a raincoat and lift the hood over my head. It's not far to the studio but the rain has shown up, and is spilling in sheets off the verandah's sloping tin roof.

I walk to the studio every morning, rarely seeing or speaking to a soul. I watch the sky above me dissolve into day – clouds vanishing, reassembling – and I try to let go of whatever has disrupted my sleep, because there's always something. If it's not the foxes prowling the chook shed or the pesky roos nosing around the bins, it's the rush of sweat that now soaks my chest at three am. I mop it off with the sheet and can usually get back to sleep, but not always. Some nights I just lie awake staring into the half-light for what feels like days, years, even, my mind turning thoughts over and over until I lose all control and they hurtle like boulders down hills in all directions. I'll be forty-six this year, so I know what it means. What my body is telling me is coming. Or going.

I hurry down the stone steps and along the soaking brick path, stopping briefly at the plum tree by my front gate. The fruit is nowhere near ripe yet – still too yellow and sour – but I steal a few anyway from spindly arms that are shaking in the rain, and drop them into my pocket to eat later. In the soggy mud at the base of the tree I spot a growing pile of rotting plums – puckered skin, burst flesh, blotches of greenish-white mould covering the fruit like soft fur – rejected by the parrots, who peck a few holes in them and then spit them to the ground. Like most creatures who know too well their own beauty, the birds here are perverse; they waste what they want, without remorse. I've yelled at them and thrown rocks. I've tried netting the tree. Nothing makes any difference. The plums never survive long enough to sweeten.

Lowering my head against the rain, I dash down the hill towards my studio – or, as locals know it better, the old stone church. The place was derelict when I bought it ten years ago – inhabited only by rats and the odd feral goat. No one had prayed in there for decades. Still, a bishop had to come all the way from Sydney to deconsecrate the place with his chants and incense before I was allowed to move in with my easel and paints. The spire is missing and all but two of the pews are gone, but the cedar beams crisscrossing the ceiling and the arched metal windows are all original. Dark patterned carpet once covered the floorboards, which I know because I saw it in a black and white photograph in the general store, and even that photo's not there anymore. Someone replaced it with a poster of Elvis in a sparkly white and gold jumpsuit.

I cut through the vacant acre of dead grass that's bordered on one side by a crumbling stone wall, and has a metal sign pegged into the ground informing tourists that *Mrs O'Dea's Ladies' Academy stood on this very spot during the gold rush*. I like to imagine them here – a class of adolescent girls in white high-necked dresses pacing the floor with books piled on their heads, or seated in neat rows conjugating verbs in French: *je vois, tu vois, il voit, elle voit* . . .

Sometimes I think I can hear them, the pretty voices of the long dead. Mingling like tree roots with the deeper ancient ones, which left the gold untroubled in the ground. But it's just the murmuring of the wind trapped low in the valley and floating up.

I cross the empty road, avoiding the black balls of scat left in mounds by the roos on the silvery-wet asphalt. Up ahead, I see the back of my studio, its knobbly stone walls impervious to the rain. As I rush to it, I think about which of my drawings I'll spend the day working up into a painting, or which of my paintings I might scrape back, or paint out completely, or turn upside-down and start again. I always try to make a plan for my eight hours in the studio, even if I ignore it once I get there. Four empty walls plus a stack of blank canvases minus any idea of how to fill them equals a demoralising place to be.

I swing open the arched front door that is treacherously low and clips my head if I'm not concentrating, and step inside. My studio is never locked. There are only my paintings to steal, and who in town would bother? (My firewood at the cottage, on the other hand, routinely goes missing if I'm not paying attention.) I peel off my sopping raincoat and shake it off, then hang it on the back of a wooden chair to dry. My drenched work boots leave muddy prints on the floor as I drag out the electric heater and plug it in. It crackles and drips as the oil inside rushes to warm up.

For a while, I stare at a half-finished painting I'm not happy with: a Bald Hill landscape I've been working on for days and can't seem to resolve. The whole thing feels too tight, too congested; and, oddly enough, as though something is still missing.

I should put it aside, I think, and not waste any more time on it. Accept it as a failure and move on with something else. Still, I keep staring at it, seeing the parts that work. The patches of airy colour I like and that it seems a shame to lose. Only I'm not sure if I can be bothered getting back into it, if it will be worth the hours I'll need to spend to find my way inside it again. To take it apart, piece by piece, and sort out what can be shed and what remains unfinished.

I lift the canvas onto my easel, a cheap replaceable thing that easily folds into a box I like to carry with me down to the river, or up to one of the lookouts, when the weather's kinder and I feel like painting outside.

I pick out a few paint tubes and start squeezing blobs of colour, so fresh they shine, onto my palette: yellow ochre, cobalt blue, lots of titanium white.

I don't wait for inspiration. It can't be relied on to come. I just take a brush and start mixing paint.

When I lived here with Clem, we made most of our paintings behind the cottage in the corrugated iron shed that's now home to the chooks. There was hardly any space compared to his studio in the city. But to me, having only ever painted in my tiny suburban bedroom, or else the busy art rooms at college, everything we needed seemed to fit: an easel and a chair each, a table for tools and brushes and paints, a stack of stretchers of various sizes, and six rolls of expensive Belgian linen Clem's father had given us both as a gift. I've always made paintings small enough to hook under one arm, and Clem's were nothing like the wall-to-wall epics he's famous for now. We seemed to be so in tune and to have so much in common; it never occurred to me it might not work. Or that in some way, beyond the physical, the two of us might not fit.

If I let myself, I can still see us here that summer, working beside each other in the shed. The air thick and stifling below the blistering tin roof; our heads starting to spin from the oil paint fumes and the violent odour of the turps. Our paintbrushes slipping from our sweaty hands. Me, on my chair, laughing at the absurdity of the situation. Clem, at his easel, telling me it wasn't funny. Me, unable to stop, delirious, telling him that it was. Him tossing a cup of days-old inky water at me to shut me up. Me tossing my own cup of dirty water back at him. The two of us locking eyes and immediately thinking the same thing; scrambling around the chairs and table, racing each other out of the shed, across the backyard, the sun thumping above us, our bare feet burning on the grass. Clem getting there first, twisting the tap, pointing the hose. Water shooting onto my back, my chest, my legs; glittering arcs of it streaking the air, flickering and falling around me like a shower of stars, saturating me as I ran in circles until I was out of breath, my soaked painting shirt clinging to me as I held up my arms, surrendering.

TWO

The blue caravan, water-soluble pencil on paper, 28 × 38 cm

It was Clem, calling to make arrangements.

I knew it was stupid to imagine he could see me, wrapped in a towel I'd grabbed from the plastic washing basket as I darted from the shower to the kitchen to answer the phone before it rang out, expecting it was him – or hoping. (Hadn't he said he'd call on Friday, not Saturday morning? And hadn't I purposely not left the flat in case I missed his call?) Still, I felt foolish and exposed. And as though Clem, without being in the room, had the power to see all of this.

It made no sense. Clem and I spoke to each other all the time at college. Before and after Life Drawing classes on Tuesday mornings and Thursday afternoons. During lunchbreaks in the leafy courtyard outside the painting studio. Plenty of times when I'd been waiting for the bus outside the towering college gates and he'd walked past, wearing his boots and leather jacket and smoking a cigarette, on his way to his beloved old cream Mercedes in the tutors' carpark.

But talking to him now, in my towel and wet feet, on the wall-mounted telephone in our dreary kitchen, with my mother's dirty dishes from the night before still stewing in the sink, and a fishy odour seeping from her discarded Thai takeaway containers, felt awkward. As if an invisible border were being crossed. Only I couldn't tell if Clem was the one crossing it, or me.

'How about we start at nine,' he said. 'Unless that's too early?'

'No, nine's perfect.'

'You sure? I haven't completely forgotten what it's like to be an undergrad. But there's no point you getting here all useless and hungover after a wild Saturday night. It's a long day. Sitting's harder work than it looks.'

'I never have wild Saturday nights,' I said, which was true. Most nights I either stacked shelves under the artificial light of the local supermarket or went to bed early so I could be up again at dawn to sketch the sky above my street as it morphed from iron-grey to dusty yellow. Then for some reason I added, 'I'm too boring.'

Clem made a small noise, not quite a laugh but something close to one, and I imagined his lips curling into a smile at the other end of the phone line, his meaty fingers scratching the brown stubble on his cheek the way he did in class when he was searching for something constructive to say to a student whose work had lost its way, or was plain bad. So I laughed too, hoping that instead of sounding nervous and immature I'd come across as casual and offhand. Confident enough to make a joke that I was dull.

But why had I called myself boring when it was the opposite of how I hoped Clem saw me? Clem, with his glittering career and renowned father and glamorous friends. I wanted to take that word back, erase it, like a line I'd drawn in the wrong place; an ill-considered mark that upset the whole picture.

I'd always been quiet, I knew that. At high school I sat on my own at the side of each class, never raising my hand even when I knew the answers to questions. My reports always praised my high marks and diligent, self-sufficient nature, but urged me to speak up more in lessons, which I'd never done. When I had to speak, my voice was timid and faint, and my teachers would ask me to repeat myself to hear what I'd just said. The other kids, deciding I was too weird or too much effort (if they thought about me at all), collectively left me alone.

Nothing much changed when I went to art school. By then most people my age were leaving home and renting cheap terraces in the city with half a dozen friends. But I still lived in a flat with my mother (who I barely saw, except when she came home from work, before she closed herself in her room to watch endless TV shows), even when I was almost twenty-one and in my third and final year of a Fine Arts degree.

No one at college ever asked me to move in with them, which was no surprise given my social life was pitiful. Even when I'd get invited (not often) to cool student share-house parties in grungy parts of the city, I'd rarely go. Socialising required too much energy. A single night out making conversation with people I hardly knew, who were either tripping on acid or too stoned to form a complete sentence, and having to pretend I was enjoying it, would leave me depleted for a week. Like an emptied fridge buzzing cool blue air onto bare shelves. I preferred to stay home in my bedroom and paint.

'Boring's not a word I'd use to describe you, Frances,' Clem said.

'No?'

'Talented's the one that comes to mind.'

'You're my teacher, you have to say that.'

'Do I?'

He was walking while he was talking to me. I could hear his heavy work boots climbing a set of stairs.

'Frighteningly talented, if you really want to know.'

I laughed.

'Nothing about me is frightening.'

Clem made that smiling sound again, breathy and unhurried, as if he had all the time in the world. As if he had nothing better to do than wander up to his incredible studio I'd seen pictures of in art magazines, and deliberate over adjectives to describe me, a nobody art student he taught twice a week at college.

'Hardworking. How's that? Better word?'

'Not much. Pretty close to boring actually.'

'Shit. I'm not doing well here.'

I heard him push a key into a lock and turn it. A door clicked open. From then on, everything he said carried a slight echo. Or maybe I just remember it that way. As though I were hearing everything twice.

'Am I allowed to say beautiful? I mean, it goes without saying. You know how you look. But . . . maybe I shouldn't say it?'

I twisted the telephone cord around my fingers, watching their tips turn reddish-white as I waited for him to say more. But instead he went silent, perhaps reconsidering the wisdom of making such a remark to a student nineteen years his junior on a private telephone out of school hours. There were rules about this sort of thing. Not that Clem was one to ever follow the rules.

'Still there?'

'Yes.'

'Have I made things awkward?'

I wanted the conversation to end. It felt as if the ground had given way beneath me. As though the floor, the phone, the dirty dishes in the sink, everything in the dismal two-bedroom flat I had lived in with my mother since I was six years old had turned to water and I was sinking in it, soundlessly, my body unresisting, my limbs splayed, my hair twisting above me like reeds.

And yet I wanted Clem to go on. I think I craved that more than anything. For his voice to sing me down deeper into the murky liquid; for his words to submerge me. Subsume me. Not that I believed half of what he was saying. Not the beautiful part, anyway. I had seen beautiful girls. Grown up next-door to them. Sat in the same classrooms as them at high school. And now, most days, I worked in painting studios alongside them at art school. Girls who floated through the world. Girls who were noticed. Girls who stole the oxygen from the air as they walked past.

I wasn't one of them, I knew that. I was more acutely aware of my flaws – physical and otherwise – than anyone: a plain pale face, my mother's swamp-green eyes, a small turned-up nose, a too-full bottom lip that would keep me looking like a child until I was ninety, and breasts so small it was a joke I bothered to wear bras (often I just went without). But I liked my hair, which was long and brown, with a fringe that fell over my eyes. I was never tempted to cut or dye it, even when everyone else at college was colouring theirs purple or green, or getting dreadlocks, or shaving their heads completely bald. My hair was one thing about me I actually liked.

'You'll be a good figure to paint,' Clem said finally, breaking the silence. But his tone had altered, shifted gears, as if he'd decided he was the teacher again and I was the student. It troubled me, even then, how easily he could change the atmosphere between us, returning us to our rightful sides like chess pieces on a board.

'And you're doing me a huge favour,' he said. 'None of my regular models can make it.'

He must have turned on a stereo at some point because I could hear Nick Drake's *Pink Moon* playing in the background. Clem had told me at the start of term, when we had first found ourselves alone in the courtyard after a class, that it was one of his favourite albums – in his top five if he were ever stranded on a desert island – and I had rushed out that afternoon and bought it on tape, never having heard of Nick Drake or his music. ('You've been missing out,' Clem had said, brushing my fringe from my eyes with his fingers.) I listened to the whole album that night, over and over in my bedroom while I painted. The plaintive guitar, the shy melancholy voice. And in my mind I saw Clem, painting too, in his proper artist's studio, smearing dark paint onto white canvas with his bare hands.

But I also saw mountains and a snaking river and a boundless sky. I saw chalky blues and fragile whites. And I saw pink.

'I already gave you the code, right? To let yourself in?'

'If I haven't lost it,' I said, quickly digging around in my brown leather satchel, which was sitting on the kitchen bench among the chaos of my mother's unpaid bills and gossip magazines, even though I knew I hadn't let the slip of paper out of my sight since Tuesday, when Clem had handed it to me after class. I'd put it straight into my diary and checked it more obsessively than I cared to admit over the intervening days, making sure it hadn't inexplicably changed or somehow vanished. But there it was, pressed to the inside cover of my diary: four numbers in black ink written in Clem's large, hectic scrawl.

An artist's handwriting reveals a lot about them, a lecturer had told us in first year, displaying an example on an overhead projector of Lucian Freud's spiky, childish print: capital letters jutting blithely from the centres of words; capitals stranded in the middles of sentences; letters slanting left bumping up against letters slanting right. I remember feeling anxious about what my small bunched-up cursive gave away about me.

'1402?' I said.

'That's it. Just punch it into the keypad when you get here and I'll buzz you up.'

'Okay.'

'See you tomorrow. Nine o'clock. No hangover.' He was about to hang up.

'Clem?'

I still felt awkward using his first name. It felt clumsy in my mouth, as if I were somehow pretending or telling a lie. At college we addressed our tutors by their surnames. But Clem had insisted on the first day that we drop it, saying it was a dumb, archaic rule, like most of the rules at art school, and that he'd agreed to being a guest lecturer for a year but not to being a wanker. 'There's enough wankers here already,' he'd said wryly. The whole class had laughed at that, even me.

'Yeah?' he said. He sounded distracted. I heard a paint lid pop open and realised he must have hooked the phone between his shoulder and his ear so he could get on with work. I was interrupting him now. Probably annoying him. Getting in his way.

'Nothing, only . . . What should I wear?'

'Whatever you like. Don't mind.'

'But do you want . . . I don't know. A particular look?'

Clem laughed then and there was no question.

'The clothes won't matter, Frances. All I'll be painting is you.'

=

Clem never remembered the first time we met.

He remembered the second time as the first, which was on day one of the Life Drawing class in third year, when he ignored the good leather swivel chair intended for him at the front of the room and sat on a table in his black jeans and leather jacket, and asked us all to introduce ourselves. He wanted to know about our backgrounds and why we'd chosen to study art, and also our ideas, if we had any yet, for the major works we would need to produce for our graduating show. No one was really listening. We were all too giddy being in the same room as Clem Hughes.

I kept quiet at the back, hoping if I let everyone else speak first we might run out of time before I had to say anything. (It was a strategy, I found, that often worked.) I also felt a bit self-conscious and embarrassed, wondering if Clem would remember me. If he might recognise my face and ask if we'd met before. 'There's something familiar about you,' I imagined him saying, the whole class turning around and looking at me in bewilderment, registering for the first time that I was there.

Clem's natural ease in front of a room full of strangers shouldn't have surprised me, but still I found it staggering. He was like an actor on stage, his gestures assured, his words utterly confident – no doubt, no hesitation – as though he were speaking lines that had been written for him already.

He relished being watched, that much was obvious; unlike me, he drew energy from it, fed off other people's attention as if it were fuel. And he seemed oblivious to the buzz in the room that a practising artist of his reputation and heritage, not to mention his relative youth (all our other tutors wore tweed and berets, or scarves tied complicatedly around their heads to hide their white hair), would be teaching us in our final year.

I was the last student to speak. And I was so unnerved by Clem's presence that my voice began to fail like an overheated car engine as soon as I stood up. With my eyes glued to the vinyl floor that I only noticed in that moment had been freshly scrubbed over the summer, I gave my name, said something about liking to paint landscapes, and sat back down again.

'Sorry – it's Frances?' Clem said, leaning forward a little.

I nodded.

'Well that was short and sweet.'

Everyone else in the class had talked about themselves for so long Clem had been forced to politely wrap them up. But my ten-second speech appeared to have confused him. For a moment he just stared at me, his dark eyes curious, attempting to make sense of mine.

'So you're into landscapes?' he said, hooking one leg over the other and exposing a rip at the knee of his jeans.

I nodded again. It was clear he didn't remember me.

'That's a fighting word, you know – landscapes – in a life drawing class.'

A petite and bosomy blonde-haired girl named Mimi, who had never directed a word at me in the two years we'd both been at college, and who was sitting curled like a cat at Clem's feet, wearing a black crochet dress and Doc Martens boots, erupted with laughter. She had spent the lesson laughing that way at everything Clem said.

Life Drawing was a compulsory unit; I wasn't doing it by choice. The human body seemed a limited subject to me. And one that had been done to death. Was there any need for yet another picture of a naked woman reclining insouciantly on a chaise longue? Or gazing at herself, bare-breasted and pensive, in a bathroom mirror? Or draped across a crumpled bed, her arms and legs languidly spread? But Clem had promised to supply us with a range of models – males as well as females, and older ones too, whose lived-in bodies might be more interesting to draw – saying he knew plenty through his own practice. And I appreciated that time spent concentrating on figures could only strengthen my observational and drawing skills. As in all subjects, I wanted to do well.

'I'd like to hear more sometime,' Clem said, glancing at the clock on the back wall and perhaps realising he was almost out of time. 'About why you're drawn to landscapes. And what it is you're trying to say.'

'I'm not trying to say anything.'

Clem stared at me again, his eyes so still and penetrating I thought I must have offended him or come across as difficult, neither of which was my intention.

'I just like painting, that's all,' I said, almost apologetically.

Clem shifted on the table, unhooking his legs. His studded black boots, I noticed, were scuffed as a schoolboy's.

'Every artist is trying to say something with their work, Frances. Even if they don't know what it is yet. Or haven't found their own language. But there's got to be a point to it, right? A bigger issue we're trying to get at, a statement we want to make. Or else what are we doing? Pushing paint around a canvas to pass the time?'

I didn't agree.

Why couldn't you make a painting for the sake of it? For the simple pleasure of it. Why did there have to be a meaning or a message? Why couldn't you look out your window or walk out your front door, and paint what you saw there in front of you every day? Capture it for no other reason than the fact it was there, existing, in that single unrepeatable moment.

Those were the artists I looked up to and hoped I could one day be like: the ones who painted by feel and instinct, who were more interested in emotion than meaning, and whose subjects were simple, quotidian, like a road or a tree. Painters like Clarice Beckett, whose quiet and, to me, foreboding works – of blurry beaches and indistinct streets, of failing light and drizzly, disappearing days – I would stand in front of for hours at the state gallery, returning to them so often I began to feel they heard me coming, whispered 'hello' as I walked up the gallery steps. To me, Clarice's misty Melbourne landscapes had no agenda, no hidden motive, no grand plan besides a true observation of colour and light. Of nature and time. Of the unremarkable streets and bays and clifftops she walked along, alone, every day. The smoky pinks, opaque blues, muted greens and vaporous greys that hang over her work like a fog – these were not dreamed up for effect or contrived to make a political point. These were her everyday reality. The ordinary, seemingly unexceptional scenes where she found impermanence, solitude, beauty.

I'd dug out everything there was to find in the college library about Clarice Beckett, which amounted, frustratingly, to very little; a few short paragraphs here and there, and two poor black and white reproductions. She, like so many other female artists of her time, had been largely overlooked in the weighty cloth-bound tomes on our college shelves. Much like her paintings, I came to feel, the details of Clarice Beckett's life were shadowy and elusive, obscure and haunting, veiled in a grey haze of mystery. I was determined to find out everything I could about her – back then I believed it would bring me closer to her work – but so little detail was ever recorded. Deliberately or not, Clarice was an artist in hiding.

All I had was a glimpse of her, an outline, a simple pencil sketch that I tried to build up into a detailed colour portrait. Clarice was a young single woman in the twenties, more interested in painting than in being a wife (she turned down several marriage proposals), and who cared for her elderly parents until she died of double pneumonia at the age of forty-eight. I read she'd asked her father for permission to use a spare room in their home as a painting studio, but that he'd refused and told her the kitchen table would do. So Clarice resolved to paint outside, en plein air, using a wooden painting trolley she built herself – a makeshift mobile easel that cleverly carried her brushes and paints. She pushed it through morning wind and evening rain, up the overcast streets and down the windy beaches of suburban Beaumaris. But only ever at dusk or dawn, for these were the strict times she was allowed. Those fleeting, ethereal hours at the edges of the day when few people were about. When, I imagined, her parents would not call her for some household chore. When the seaside light was washy and still forming, or blearily fading away.

Critics at the time – unanimously male – complained Clarice's work was too soft, too fuzzy, too weak, too dreary, too flat. I wondered if any of them considered how dreary and flat her life was; how limited and prescribed it was, even down to the diaphanous times of day she was permitted to paint. And how, if she'd had any message at all as an artist, any meaning behind her paintings, that might have been it.

But I knew that saying any of this out loud to Clem and the class would only provoke an argument and draw the moment out. Where I saw Clarice as a radical modernist – an Australian landscape painter ahead of her time – others dismissed her as a conservative lady painter of pretty, lightweight, ultimately insignificant pictures. So I nodded instead, keeping my thoughts, as usual, to myself.

Clem smiled, happy I appeared to agree with him, and hopped down off the table. He said he'd see us all next week, and we'd hit the ground running with a life model. Mimi rushed up to talk to him before he left the room, the tiny holes in her crochet dress offering a clear view of her figure. I picked up my satchel and left for my next class, not looking at Clem again. It was hardly the most memorable exchange.

But Clem told me many months later, when the two of us were lying for the first time on the pillowy day bed in his studio, my pink dress abandoned somewhere on the floor, the afternoon sun coating our worn-out bodies with pearly light, that I had stood out to him from the start.

'You were the only one there who seemed like a real artist. Like it really meant something to you. The others were all talk,' he said, his paint-stained fingers tracing the curve of my hip, the nook of my waist, the inner crevice of my thigh. 'I knew you were good straightaway.'

The doors would open at six pm. I knew that much without having seen an invite. I'd been dropping in on Porter Street Gallery's monthly exhibition openings ever since I started art school two years ago (it was only three blocks away) and they always started at six. You could also rely on there being a team of waiters dressed head to toe in black, carrying trays of complimentary wine and even champagne if the artist showing was a particularly old or revered one. At Porter Street, they tended to be both.

It wasn't much of a gallery to look at: a three-storey brown brick terrace on a quiet corner block in Paddington, with musty beige carpet, low ceilings and a steep wooden staircase that had claimed more than a few drunken art collectors in its time. The gallery door was half obscured by a sprawling jacaranda tree that, towards the end of each spring, left a carpet of mauve blossoms on the footpath below. The place looked less like an art gallery and more like a well-to-do old bachelor's dated, sleepy home. It was nothing like the sleek contemporary art spaces made of concrete and glass that showcased cutting-edge artists under track lighting in fringe locations around the city you needed a map to find. But Porter Street was uninterested in moving with the times or updating itself in any way, choosing instead to hold firmly to its roots.

I never saw any other students from college there. It wasn't much of a student scene. Porter Street was old school. The artists gave speeches – long and rambling ones – about their life, their work, their friendships and feuds with other artists, their winding trails of ex-wives and lovers and children, and their grudges against art critics who had perniciously picked apart their paintings and still failed to understand them – and invariably signed off by passionately declaring they would be devoted to the brush until they could no longer hold one in their hand. The people on Porter Street's mailing list, or at least the ones I observed at openings, were not cool or fashionable or young. They were serious and seasoned art collectors: moneyed, opinionated, entitled, traditional.

But tonight the mood was different. And the people walking into the gallery looked different too. There was the usual neat crowd of elderly couples in navy blazers and pearls, and women of a certain age dressed in shapeless print kaftans and chunky necklaces. But just behind them, descending on the gallery with intent, was a wave of young people. Polished thirty-somethings in stilettos and pencil skirts, or tailored suits and ties, who looked like they'd just left work at a classy law firm or an advertising agency. I glanced down at my own clothes: my denim overalls and cardigan from Vinnies, my worn painting boots, my mother's green opal engagement ring that she said was too ugly and gaudy to wear but that I liked, my brown leather satchel stuffed with drawing books and pencils that I carried with me everywhere. I worried I would stand out for all the wrong reasons.

I considered walking back to the bus stop. I could see the exhibition another time when there were fewer – and less intimidating – people to contend with; when I'd have a better chance of seeing the paintings unobstructed, instead of having to glimpse them over the tops of people's heads. A jam-packed opening, like this one was shaping up to be, was a frustrating way to view an artist's work, and hardly worth the effort. But I'd heard a rumour at college that Clem Hughes was going to be one of our third-year tutors and I was curious to see his work in the flesh. So I held my satchel close, mindful not to bump anyone with it, and moved inside.

I'd read about Clem Hughes. His stellar career had been recorded in every newspaper and art magazine you cared to name. (Only the week before, I'd seen him on the cover of *Art Circle* wearing a black designer suit, no shirt, a loose bow tie draped around his neck, feet bare, sitting on an antique armchair splattered with paint.) The articles were always accompanied by photographs of his work, but just as often they featured his studio – an enormous three-storey converted warehouse in the city with five-metre-high white walls and four hundred square metres of concrete floor, most of it stained with oil paint – where he made his dark and controversial works. Sometimes the articles also showed a black and white photograph of Clem as a little boy in striped shorts and leather sandals, a bowl cut, a bare bony chest. He is sitting cross-legged on the floor and staring up at his father, four-time Archibald winner Albert Hughes, who is standing at an easel painting one of his stirring portraits that became the stuff of Australian art legend.

But Clem's paintings had none of the masterly control, nothing of the sumptuous, jewel-like palette or the contemplative, disciplined approach that were the well-loved signatures of his father's. As I now saw, having carved a path through the loud crowd to stand directly in front of one of the dozen or so paintings on show, Clem's work was disturbing. Sinister. Chaotic. Painted primarily in black and white, in a stark, aggressive style that fell somewhere between realism and abstraction – neither paintings nor drawings but some crashing together of the two, like voices hurled across a room in an argument.

A whirl of nude female forms, slack-bodied and still-eyed, expressionless, their carcass-like figures overlapping and merging into each other like melted wax. Coalescing heads, as if seen with double-vision or caught, frame by frame, in rapid movement. Roughly sketched arms and legs, the hands and feet vanishing eerily into thin drips. Disembodied bits of breast and elbow and thigh, and other unidentifiable body parts, rendered in oil paint that still carried a potent smell. These were paintings that threatened to eat up the very walls they were hanging on. I felt a violence when I looked at them. A fierce and roaring lack of restraint, an anger and recklessness that terrified me. Clem's paintings were like nightmares.

I found it hard to reconcile the paintings with the man, who was shifting about the room from one cluster of admirers to another. His dark wavy hair flopped onto his cheeks and shoulders, his face was tanned and sparkling, sporting an easy smile, as if he'd just stepped out of the Mediterranean. His complexion was more olive than I'd understood from pictures, and he looked shorter, with a broad chest and bulky shoulders that seemed out of proportion to the rest of him, as if they'd been stuck on by mistake. He was wearing a brown suede waistcoat over a shirt with the top buttons left undone, and jeans that had been splashed up the legs with coloured paint (whether deliberately or not, I couldn't tell). On anyone else, it would have seemed a pretentious outfit. And maybe it was. Except Clem managed to look entirely comfortable and relaxed, unconcerned with himself, as though he'd simply put on whatever clothes he'd found first, with no thought to the fact that he was dressing for his opening at Porter Street, a gallery that had never before deigned to show a living artist under the age of forty.

Was it possible Clem was unaware of the things people said about him? That he hadn't heard the gossip I had heard at college? The snide rumours, spread between the lines of fawning articles and reviews, that he was only showing at Porter Street because of his famous father. That the gallery could hardly have said no to representing the son of the acclaimed artist who had helped make it rich. That without the sway of his illustrious surname, Clem would never get away with charging five figures a painting, and that anyone unwise enough to buy one better be prepared to watch its value dive on the secondary market. That his works were ugly, obvious, lazy, misogynistic, unhinged; the wails of a traumatised child still grieving his lost mother. That as a painter Clem lacked skill and technique. That he had no aptitude for drawing. That he avoided painting hands and faces because they were the hardest parts to get right and he was copping out. That he had nothing in his arsenal besides shock. That no matter how hard he tried, he would never be half the artist his father was. That if he wasn't the son of national treasure Albert Hughes, Clem's painting career would already be over.

'Thinking of buying one?'

A large man wearing a grey felt hat had positioned himself beside me. I could smell his woody cologne.

'There's still one or two over there that don't have red dots,' he said, pointing at the wall behind us. 'But I suggest you run.'

He was holding a catalogue and a price list. I saw a gold signet ring on his pinky finger.

'Just looking,' I said.

'Famous last words,' he smirked, his teeth too white to be natural. He had a wide face with thick rumpled skin that looked as if it had been kneaded into shape by the ungainly fingers of a child.

'Over here,' he called to a waitress who was passing with a tray. 'This young lady's missing a drink.'

The waitress looked bored and compliant. She stopped and held out the tray.

'Red or white?' the man asked benevolently, as if the wine were his own.

'White. Thanks,' I said, more to the waitress than to him.

'Cin cin.' He handed me a glass, then clinked it with another he'd picked up for himself.

I took a sip and turned back to the painting, hoping if I didn't make eye contact and said nothing more he'd move away. Something about him filled me with a sense of dread. But instead he stepped closer. I could feel his eyes taking in my long messy hair, my second-hand clothes, my bulky satchel, my cheap boots that I only in that moment noticed had a dot of blue paint on one toe.

'Are you an artist?' he asked.

'Art student.'

'Ahhh.' He nodded, impressed with himself for guessing near the mark. 'Then you know a good painting when you see one?'

I shrugged.

'Tell me, what do you think of that one over there, by the stairs?'

He was pointing to one of the smallest paintings in the show. About sixty by fifty centimetres, it featured a pair of intertwined nude female figures with creepy faceless heads that seemed to stare out soullessly from the canvas, though they had no eyes.

'Best work in the show or what?'

It was not a good painting. In fact, I thought it was the weakest and least resolved of all. Too cursory and slapdash, too lopsided in its composition, and the blacks too flat. I got the sense it had been painted in a hurry, as an afterthought, perhaps when someone at the gallery realised they were short a work to fill the space by the stairs. I felt sure that if you touched the surface, the paint below the membrane would still be liquid.

Stuck to the wall below the painting was a small red dot indicating it was sold.

'Is it yours?' I asked, figuring it must be.

The man grinned proudly, his white teeth wolfish as he leaned uncomfortably close to my ear.

'Just bought it,' he whispered, his hot breath brushing the side of my neck. Then he tipped his head back and swallowed a mouthful of wine, as if rewarding himself for some remarkable achievement. I wondered if this had been his purpose in talking to me all along. If owning a piece of art and hanging it up on your wall – or simply telling a stranger it was yours – could feel as gratifying as having made it yourself.

'Congratulations,' I said, assuming this was what he wanted.

'I have another one at home. From Clem's last show in Brisbane. Did you see it?'

'No,' I said. 'I've never been to Brisbane.'

The man winced as if I'd injured him.

'Fuck, it was powerful. That's all I can say. And look,' he went on, 'I know his work's not for everyone. Even I wouldn't hang it in my bedroom. Or maybe this one, I would. What do you think?' He smiled greasily and cupped my elbow, leaning close again, his shoulder touching mine. 'But get yourself onto his mailing list, quick smart. Mine have already doubled in value. I should have bought twenty.'

I shifted my elbow and, as if understanding, the man let go and turned back to the painting. In the silence that hung between us as we stared ahead at Clem's work, the boisterous chatter in the room seemed to grow louder and more hysterical, until it felt as if the gallery itself were mocking me, reminding me I had no place within its walls. I looked at my watch. If I ran half the way, I would make the next bus home.

I didn't know what to do with my glass of wine so I downed it and made a move for the door. I had no idea if the man was still watching me, thinking I was rude or aloof, and I didn't care. I just wanted to leave. But there were so many people now crammed into the gallery I couldn't see a clear way out. I excused myself over and over, squeezing past people shrieking at each other to be heard above all the noise. The room felt manic, like a small cage at a zoo heaving with too many animals. I could feel sweat pooling in my armpits and my face turning red, but there was no space to take off my cardigan. I regretted throwing down the wine; my empty stomach was now gurgling. I had to get outside. I needed air. I pushed my way forward, shoving past anyone standing between me and the door.

'Sorry, are you trying to get out?'

Clem was only an inch taller than me. Our eyes were almost level and, at this moment, awkwardly close. I hadn't realised the person I had been trying to push past was him.

'Yes,' I think I said.

Clem reached for my hand as if he knew it. As if he'd reached for it a thousand times before. I felt his fingers grip my palm and lead me forward. I followed without question, walking wordlessly, the crowd instinctively parting to let us through. Every few steps a voice would call out to him, or a hand would reach out and touch him, urging him to stop. But it was as though Clem didn't notice, or didn't want to, or else had some rare brand of confidence assuring him they would all still be there, waiting for him, wanting him, whenever he chose to come back.

A wave of cool air and cigarette smoke hit my face as we stepped onto the footpath outside. The sun that had been setting when I arrived had disappeared, and in its place was a petrol-blue sky. Dozens of people had spilled out of the gallery and were standing among the shiny cars parked on the street. Or maybe they hadn't braved entering yet, and were waiting for others to leave.

I felt Clem's hand release mine. I hadn't realised I was still holding onto it.

'Better out here?'

I nodded. 'Thanks,' I managed to say.

He took the empty wineglass from my hand and threw it into someone's hedge. We were standing in the dark, I realised, away from the glowing streetlights and where, it only occurred to me as I was riding the night bus home, Clem could be anonymous for a few minutes.

'You looked like you were about to pass out,' he said.

'I felt like it.'

'Thought I'd have to catch you for a second.'

He took a pack of cigarettes and a lighter from his jeans pocket. I watched him flick a cigarette out of the pack, place it between his lips and light it. Then he offered one to me.

'Thanks, I don't smoke.'

I peeled off my cardigan. My armpits were soaking and I worried I smelled awful. I took a step backwards just in case.

'Was it my paintings, was it?' Clem asked, blowing out smoke and waving it away from me.

'Sorry?'

'That made you almost pass out.'

'No. But they're gruesome enough to do that.'

'Shit.' He laughed, flicking away some ash. 'Lucky you're not writing my review.'

'Sorry, I didn't mean to—'

'No, it's good,' he said. 'I think it's a compliment.' He took another drag on his cigarette. 'That's how you know you've really made it in the art world. When you're knocking people unconscious with your work.'

I couldn't tell if he was joking or not. I watched him glance back at the gallery, where people were still jostling at the door, even though it seemed impossible another body could fit inside.

'Are your openings always like this?' I asked.

Clem shrugged, as though he were the last person on the planet responsible for the madness in front of us, or able to make any sense of it. He tossed his cigarette to the ground and squashed it with his boot.

'There's so many people here,' he said, 'that I really couldn't be fucked talking to.' His dark eyes were slack and glassy from too much wine. He sighed. 'But maybe don't put that in your review.'

I remember thinking in that moment that I liked his face. The rich warm colour of it. The deep vertical lines that sat between his heavy eyebrows, one extending a little higher than the other. And the softer creases at his temples that bent down towards his cheekbones, as though someone had neatly drawn them on.

'You're okay now? Not going to keel over? Don't want to find you later in the hedge.'

I felt myself smiling, blushing.

'I'm fine.'

He nodded and without another word began walking back to the gallery, his hands pushed deep into his pockets, his shoulders slightly hunched, his figure seeming to shrink beneath the yellow brightness of the streetlights. As he neared the gallery door, a tall bald guy with a full-sleeve tattoo and a stunning redhead I recognised as a television actress (she was on some of the covers of my mother's magazines) reached out and grabbed him.

'Nailed it, man!' said the guy, punching Clem's arm with affection.

'But what the hell, they're all sold,' complained the redhead, kissing then hugging him. 'Do I need to camp out next time to get one?'

Standing alone on the dark footpath, I watched Clem exchange a few more words with them then slip back into the gallery. In a matter of seconds he was swallowed up by the mass of people and I could no longer see him.

It should have been clear to me in that moment how unequal we were. How misaligned. I was not born of art royalty like Clem. My father was an angry drunk who left without a word when I was small, not one of the country's most celebrated living artists. My mother was a depressed suburban receptionist who spent ten hours a day sitting at the front desk of a second-hand car yard, not a bohemian French–Moroccan muse. I did not have classical musicians for godparents, nor did I grow up with Nolans and Streetons on the walls. I felt I had no right to want more than a glimpse into Clem's sparkling world. But I did.

Clem never remembered helping an unsteady girl out of the gallery at his opening. Why would he? He must have talked to a few hundred people that night and consumed enough alcohol to blur most of his senses.

But that was the first time we met. The first time his fingers locked around mine and I felt that strange electric knowing. Like a pulse I had just picked up.

I've never forgotten it.

The caravan was blue.

Not dark blue, my father said. I was sitting in the passenger seat of his noisy car, the vinyl cold and slippery under my legs, still too short to reach the floor, his brown corduroy jacket with the white woolly lining, big as a blanket, spread over my lap to keep me warm. The smudgy grey moon following us, chasing us like a hopeless spy, racing past the clouds to keep up.

Blue, like the morning sky, he said. Pale and frosty. I would like it. I liked blue, didn't I? I liked colours and drawing and stuff. I was good at drawing, wasn't I? I could thank him for that.

He'd found it cheap. Everything had to be cheap now since my bitch mother had taken everything – every last cent they got from the house, and the good car with the heater, not like this useless piece of shit she had left him with. Was I warmer yet?

But the caravan, he said, was unusual. Unique. I'd like it. It used to be a library once. On wheels. How about that, Francie? With shelves on both sides and a big comfy seat up the back that folded out into a bed when you wanted it to, like magic.

Were there still books in there? I asked.

Nope, he said, no books, Francie. And no shower and no toilet and no microwave to cook dinner with, either. We'd have to use the caravan park facilities for that. But it would be fun. Like being on holiday every time I came to visit. I'd visit him, wouldn't I? I'd come and stay with him. I wouldn't believe all the bullshit lying crap my bitch mother said about him.

But when I did come – with my sleeping bag and my warm pyjamas and my clothes for the next day packed inside a plastic bag, my mother already leaving, reversing her car out the park gate, the good car with the heater – the caravan was not there.

In its place was a rectangle of dry grass. A flat patch

of absence between rows and rows of caravans that weren't my dad's.

The caravan was blue, like the sky.

Clem's eyes flicked between me and the canvas, me and the canvas. Then he made another heavy downwards mark. The long hog hair paintbrush he was using made a scratching sound, as though Clem were excavating the surface to reveal an image buried below, not building one up with layers of pigment.

There was the familiar tang of oil paint, only much stronger and more acrid than I was used to; it lodged, cold and sharp, in the back of my throat. And behind me, near one of the tall windows that lined one side of the studio, a fan hummed, turning slowly, its metal blades slicing the air. A stack of wooden stretchers sat against the back wall, waiting to be bound and stapled with the primed French linen bundled beside them in two-metre-high rolls. And drifting up from the grimy street three floors below, the muffled noise of city traffic: cars brakes screeching, horns honking, drivers swearing out their windows.

'You thought I'd make you pose naked, right?'

I tried not to smile. Or fidget. Or move. It felt as if the square wooden plinth Clem had asked me to stand on for the past three hours had grown teeth and was starting to bite. I'd been ignoring a pain in the balls of my feet for twenty minutes – or forty minutes, I could no longer tell. Time had become strangely elastic while I'd been standing on the plinth. But I was determined to hold the pose.

'And you came anyway,' he said.

He was looking at me impassively, as if I were a maths problem he needed to solve; I could feel him breaking down my features, just like he'd taught us to do in class: the face an oval, the eyes exactly halfway down, the bottom of the nose halfway between the pupils and the bottom of the chin, the middle of the mouth halfway between the bottom of the chin and the bottom of the nose.

'You're braver than I thought,' he said, striking the canvas once more with the paintbrush.

I had felt relief (and though I was ashamed to admit it, a slight sting of disappointment) when Clem had said he wanted to paint me in my pink dress, instead of nude on the day bed I saw conveniently placed beside his easel. He was inspired, he'd said, by the possibilities the dress suggested to him with its vibrant colours and busy floral pattern. Swathes of donut-icing pink. Dabs of carmine and magenta. Swirls of leafy green. Miles away from his usual narrow palette of blacks and whites. It had made him want to try a straight portrait. Or as straight as he could make one. 'If you're up for that?' he'd said. 'It might take a while.'

I had bought the dress brand new from a shop on Oxford Street I walked past every day between the bus stop and college. It was one of the few pieces of clothing I owned that hadn't come from an op shop or been an eighties' hand-me-down from my mother. The dress was expensive – too expensive to ever wear to college and risk damaging with paint; and other than my shifts at the supermarket I went hardly anywhere else. Plus I rarely wore pink; it seemed a colour for little girls. But none of that mattered when I put the dress on and saw my reflection in the shop mirror. The fitted waist gave me hips that weren't mine, the gathered bust amplified my small breasts, the dangly shoulder ties softened the sharp angles of my neck and collarbone, and the pink fabric instantly warmed my pale skin as if I'd been kissed by the sun. I didn't look like myself in it. I looked like someone else. Someone better.

My eyes, I realised, had wandered from the dent in the wall Clem had told me to stare at at the start of the session so that my gaze would stay at a constant level throughout. I told myself to concentrate. To keep my mind inside the room. To not forget that every millimetre of me was being scrutinised. I had no delusions of being a professional model – and no interest in being one either – but I wanted Clem to think I was good at this, in much the same way I wanted him to think I was good at everything.

When I'd arrived at the studio that morning we'd talked about various poses – should I stand or sit in a chair? Should he focus on my upper half or make the portrait full-length? Should I be in profile or face directly forward? – before Clem had decided on a simple standing pose with my arms hanging by my sides that he said should be easy enough to hold for a few hours. I stepped onto the plinth and he positioned me side-on to the biggest blank canvas I'd ever seen – two and a half by two metres, it towered over my head – which he'd balanced against a dark wooden easel on wheels that stood six feet tall and looked antique. Possibly, I thought, it had been Clem's father's easel once, and another artist's before that, and I was joining a long line of models to have been painted before it. As I stared at the dent in the wall, I imagined their rendered figures around me, a party of spectres: some lithe and some lumpy; some so dense and impastoed you could see the palette knife strokes up and down their flesh; others with forms as delicate and lustrous as glass.

As if I had conjured her, Clem's mother appeared among them, resplendent and goddess-like, more vivid than all the rest: her naked skin wet and glistening blue-violet, her thick hair billowing over her shoulders like spirals of dark smoke, her hooded charcoal eyes fierce and imploring, boring into mine until I felt so shaky, so unbalanced, I had to look away.

'Try to keep still,' Clem said. 'You're moving a lot.'

I found the dent again and tried to think only of that. I couldn't tell exactly where on the canvas Clem was working his brush, but from the way his eyes kept returning to mine, his forehead a knot of concentration, I guessed he was filling in the outline he'd drawn of my face: laying in the muddy greens of my irises, the blocks of shadow below my eyes and nose and cheekbones, the fleshy swell of my bottom lip. If I talked or moved right now, I would not only alter the way the light fell on my skin and confuse things for Clem, mixing up the patches of light and dark, but would also have to find my way back to this exact position, this precise expression: my head turned slightly to the right, my chin tilted upwards, my lips held in a straight line.

I had never posed for an artist before. Besides Clem, no one had ever asked me to, and if they had I'm sure I would have said no. I saw no point in standing inert for hours while someone else made a painting, when I could be making one myself instead. I was an artist, not a model. So what was I doing here? And why, I began to ask myself, had I agreed to give away my Sunday, a day I routinely spent painting, by standing in this rigid pose, inanimate as a flower or a vase?

But I knew, of course. Clem and I both knew, didn't we? Or was it all in my head?

'Right to hold there another minute?' Clem asked as he squeezed a ball of red paint onto his palette – a long wooden table with wheels, the original surface entombed below inches of dried paint – mixing it with blue and a little pink and a touch of black until it formed a rich purple colour that he thinned out with some medium. 'Then I'm done.'

I made a sound that meant yes without moving my eyes or mouth, even though I was desperate to scratch an itch on my nose and shift my feet that had gone numb. I'd never realised how much effort it took to pose for a painting. How exhausting it was to pretend all your thoughts and bodily instincts could be stilled. How parts of you were necessarily diminished, even lost, when you became two-dimensional, when you were reduced to only marks; an ancient kind of surgery.

Clem let out a long breath. Then he walked backwards and forwards in front of the canvas a couple of times, tipping his head this way and that, his face inscrutable as he assessed his work. Then he put down his brush.

'You can step down now,' he said, rubbing his eyes with the backs of his hands and stretching his arms over his head as if he'd just woken from a deep sleep. 'It's not finished yet. There's still a few things I have to work on. One of your arms isn't right – you'll see, it's too long. And I made your feet too big. I'll have to fix that. But come have a look.'

My body wouldn't move.

Was I scared to find out how Clem saw me? Or if he saw me at all? Was something terrible and hideous – some maimed and contorted version of myself – waiting for me there on the other side of the canvas? Had Clem painted me haunted and half-dead like all the nameless figures I'd seen in his paintings? Did I still have my hands? My legs? Or were they dissolving into a crude and colourless background? Had he taken all my parts and dismantled them, mixed them up like pieces of a macabre jigsaw only he knew the trick to reassembling?

'You look terrified,' Clem said.

'Just a bit stiff,' I lied. 'Not used to standing still for that long.'

Clem was watching me closely, trying to decipher me, I felt, like a foreign language he'd never encountered before.

'You don't have to be scared, Frances.'

'I'm not scared,' I said. I even smiled. But my feet still refused to move, as though they'd been cemented to the plinth.

Clem stepped towards me.

'But something's wrong. I can tell.' He sounded worried.

'If you'd asked me to pose naked, I would have.'

The words tumbled from my mouth on their own, without permission, startling me with their rawness.

But it was true. I would have done anything Clem asked, anything he wanted. It was as simple and undeniable as that. And perhaps it was this realisation – more than any horrific image he could have painted of me – that had paralysed me.

'Trust me, Frances,' Clem said, pulling off his dirty painting shirt and then his work boots, tossing them into a corner. 'The first time I see you naked, it won't be for a painting.'

And just like that, I knew it was going to happen. Maybe not this afternoon. Maybe not until after I had graduated and no one could condemn it. But there was no doubt in my mind.

Or maybe it was already happening, his mouth finding a way to mine, drawing me into him, right now.

For three whole days, I didn't leave his studio.

There was nothing I wanted or needed that wasn't already there. I didn't call my mother to tell her where I was. I didn't show up for work and I didn't ring to explain. I didn't change my clothes; I wore Clem's painting shirts and nothing else, no underwear, no shoes. I drank fancy French wine and listened to Bob Dylan for the first time, Clem mouthing to me behind the smoke of his cigarette, *You're a big girl now.* I made a nest around myself with his heavy art books, spending hours staring at the works of

Titian, Velázquez, Picasso, Schiele, Rothko, de Kooning, Freud. I hung Clem's camera around my neck and took black and white photographs of him while he painted – his chest bare, his hair tied back, one curl escaping over his eyes. I saw the amber city streetlights below us blink awake as the sky slowly darkened outside the tall studio windows. And I heard the growling garbage trucks break the morning's silence with their indifferent beeping and hissing and smashing of glass. I don't remember if I showered or ate or drank anything besides croissants and the espresso coffee Clem bought from the café across the road. I'm not sure I even slept. I didn't need to. I was running on something else.

Mostly we had sex on the day bed, but we also used an armchair, a wooden work table and, once or twice, the concrete floor. I hesitated when Clem threw down a dirty drop sheet to make it more comfortable, though not by much, and stop us from rolling on clumps of congealed paint.

'There's more paint on the drop sheet than the floor,' I said. 'We'll get it all over us.'

'Fuck. You're right.' He laughed, not caring, pulling me down.

I began to see my body the way he saw it – as a thing of supple movement and fluid lines; of verticals, horizontals, diagonals; of rising and falling forms – as a thing, I began to feel, of a sort of beauty.

I let my fingers go where he placed them. Let him watch me, photograph me, paint me exploring my own geography. I withheld nothing. I yielded everything. I slipped into him. Or he slipped into me. The lines had blurred.

His memories were cloudy, he said. Just as soon as he felt he'd caught one it would dart away, like a shy or untrusting animal, dissolving into imprecise shapes he could not keep hold of. The realness of her face – beyond the legion of representations he'd grown up with in his father's paintings – was long ago lost to him, along with the sound of her voice singing him lullabies in French, though some part of him distinctly remembered that she had, and that she sang well. His mother, Clem told me, was no more than a sunken shadow to him now. A bloated darkness. An unreachable and watery ghost.

Once again, I'd punched the numbers into the buzzer and run up the two flights of stairs to his studio. For those first few intoxicating months it was our only place. Going out together to his favourite restaurants and bars was too public, too risky. Accompanying him to the never-ending array of parties, dinners and openings he was invited to was out of the question. My bedroom had never really been an option, with my poky single bed and the likelihood of my mother finding out, though I assured Clem she wouldn't care or tell anyone, or probably even notice since she paid so little attention to what was going on in my life as it was. My mother hadn't asked me where I was suddenly spending all my time; she had simply accepted, without comment or question, that I was now hardly ever around.

But no one would be suspicious if they saw me coming or going from the studio, or so Clem convinced me, since even if one of the other tutors from college turned up unannounced and found me naked, I could well be sitting for a painting, and had in fact done so many times. More than a dozen half-finished portraits of me – some naked, some clothed, some based on photographs Clem had taken, some painted from life during hours-long sittings – hung on the back wall, along with the completed one of me in the pink dress, which was Clem's favourite. And maybe, he said, the best work he'd ever done.

'There was nothing different about that day,' Clem said to me now, as he lit a cigarette. 'Nothing that stood out or gave any hint of what she was thinking. Not to me anyway. But I was a kid, I didn't know shit about what was going on in her head. She just worked all morning and went out to buy things for lunch like she always did. Dad liked a pastry in the afternoon when he finished painting. Still does.'

Clem's head was resting on my belly and I was playing with his hair, twisting strands of it between my fingers while he smoked. I could feel the cool air from the fan latch onto the sweat dotting my ribs, just below the lacy blue bra I'd taken to wearing. Afternoon sunlight was pouring through the windows and landing on Clem's bare legs, turning them the warm glossy colour of dark honey.

'I wanted to go with her. I made a big fuss. If you were a kid and polite at the market, they'd give you things – lollies, sweets, a toy if you were lucky. But she said no, she had too much to do, she'd take me next time.'

Clem turned his face to blow out smoke as if he were hoping it would blow away the memory.

'She kissed my cheeks and told me to be a good boy. To stop crying and not be loud and bother Papa while he was working. To make her a drawing if I got bored. She was always telling me to make drawings.'

Clem squashed the last of his cigarette into the green glass ashtray beside him on the day bed. Then he pushed it away.

'I stayed there sitting at her table for hours, not making a sound, not touching her things. Just waiting. Watching for her out the window. I kept seeing people that I thought might be her . . . but she never came back.'

I felt like an imposter, lying there listening to Clem tell me about his mother. I wished I had known nothing about her – not what she looked like, not her elegant French name, not her habit of wearing silk scarves tied on one side around her neck – so that I could have come to his story cold. But Evangeline Hughes was not unknown to me.

I was as guilty as the next person of having examined the salacious bones of her story. Anyone who'd ever picked up a tabloid newspaper, let alone an art magazine, would have read how, as a gifted young artist on a prestigious travel scholarship to Paris, Albert Hughes had met and fallen in love with a beautiful, vivacious French–Moroccan sculptor eleven years his senior named Evangeline, whose sensuous and arresting semi-abstract clay figures were highly sought after in the stylish arrondissements of Paris. Her work was known for being provocative and unpredictable, and her behaviour even more so. Evangeline was impulsive, mercurial, wild. When she turned her eye to Albert – precociously talented, blue-eyed and foreign, sexually unschooled but with an appetite to learn – the two were besotted with each other instantly. In a letter home to a former art-school friend (its contents later quoted ad nauseam), Albert wrote that Evangeline was 'the most magnetic, beguiling woman I have ever met. By some stroke of grand fortune, I have found my muse.' Albert shortened her name to Eva, because when he said it the French way and got the accent right it sounded like the

English word 'ever', which was nothing short of the length of time he wanted to be with her.

Albert and Eva quickly had a son they named after her estranged father, Clément, who still lived in the hilly countryside village near Lyon where Eva had spent her childhood. The little boy grew up playing with paint and clay the way other children played with teddy bears and toy cars. It was not unusual for guests (and there were hordes of them – artists, collectors, dealers, musicians, writers, actors – at all hours of the day and night) to see him crawling along the parquet boards of Eva's rented fifth-floor apartment near the Canal Saint-Martin dressed in nothing but a cloth nappy, his plump little body and face decorated in coloured paint he'd daubed onto himself with a stray brush. Clem spoke fluent French before he could utter a word of English, a language he only began to learn when he was eight years old, after his mother's death, when Albert packed up the Paris apartment and relocated them both to a narrow grey terrace in his home city of Sydney, Australia.

Eva was the subject of countless Albert Hughes portraits, including one of her lying naked in a bath against a wall of hexagonal blue and violet tiles, the private details of her body – her nipples, her belly button, her spread of pubic hair – clearly visible below the waterline; a portrait that won him his first Archibald Prize at the age of thirty-two. Albert's *Eva* paintings were widely acknowledged to be among his most desired and valuable works. No serious art collector in the country felt their walls were complete without at least one painting of Eva's sylphic limbs and dark oblong face gazing out at them from a canvas.

I wasn't a huge fan of the *Eva* paintings – not that I would ever have said so to Albert or Clem. It was difficult to pinpoint what it was I didn't like about them or why they didn't move me more. Technically they were flawless, like all of Albert's paintings; Eva's likeness was striking and perfect, the compositions meticulously balanced, Albert's brushwork impeccable, not a stroke hurried or out of place. But perhaps Albert's faultlessness – his ruthless precision and unerring control – was part of the problem? I saw no risk in the execution, no sense of daring or even delight. To me, the *Eva* paintings were disappointingly staid and hollow. A sense of emptiness washed over me whenever I looked at them, which never failed to make me embarrassed I was getting something wrong or missing the point somehow, since I knew I was meant to be feeling something quite different: desire and longing perhaps, or sublime love. But these emotions seemed oddly absent from the canvas. Eva was nude; Eva was vulnerable and splendid in an intimate setting; Eva was there, but she was not there.

I preferred Albert's interior paintings, which he made in the years following Eva's death, of vacant and barely furnished rooms that still carried the uneasy presence of someone who had just left or was expected to arrive. Rooms that were holding their breath: the chairs unoccupied, the bookshelves bare, the walls unadorned, the doors tentatively ajar. These paintings had a tension and atmosphere Albert's portraits of Eva lacked – disquiet emanated from them like a smell, they were electrically charged, their stillness *moved* – though he made far fewer of them. A small number hung in various state galleries or were tightly held in private collections. A couple from Albert's own collection had been reproduced in monographs – one I was especially drawn to showed a large empty bedroom through a doorway, as if the viewer were perhaps too hesitant to enter, moonlight pouring through a sash window and streaking a stripped mattress on the floor pinkish-blue. But most of Albert's interiors from this time, Clem told me, remained in Albert's studio, hidden in racks, gathering dust.

'He can't look at them,' Clem said, lighting another cigarette.

That night, alone in my single bed in my mother's flat, her door closed, the drone of her television behind it, I dreamed.

As if I were there, watching them. As if I were somehow in the room with them, silent and invisible.

A cramped but delightful apartment in Paris. The walls of the chicly cluttered space salon-hung with oil paintings in ornate wooden frames, all higgledy-piggledy, none of them quite straight, as if a wind had just shot through and blown them all off-centre.

A slim and sunny front room overlooking a cobbled courtyard far below. The sound of a kitten somewhere nearby, hungry, calling.

A messy work table strewn with sculpting tools: little wooden hammers and knives. Coils of thin silver wire for building armatures. Bowls of water. Scraps of dirty rags. Heavy rectangular blocks of clay, as grey-white as bone.

A work in progress abandoned in the middle of the table. A curving, headless torso? A piece of a body in flight? An unfinished thing with Eva's fingerprints all over it.

The kitten suddenly there at the window, mottled and thin, reeking of something spoiled. Its face contorting as it mewls, its pink paws scrabbling at the air.

And Clem, so small, only a little boy, not much taller than the work table. His shaggy hair spilling over his eyes, making them difficult to see. His arms latched to his mother's leg, clinging to her, steadfast, stubborn, frightened. Making her drag him along the parquet floor as she moves to the door. Howling at her to take him with her, demanding it.

Eva swearing at him in French. Words I don't understand, but somehow do.

Her hands dry and rough from the clay she's been reshaping all morning. Her fingers coated in grey – as if already decaying – peeling Clem off.

The sound of her shoes, soft and flat, disappearing down the stairs.

He was sitting beside me, cross-legged on a blue and white striped towel, his hands blackened by the charcoal pencil he'd been using to sketch random people on the beach: a soft-bellied man sitting alone, looking out to the low horizon, his arms and legs bendy and elastic, joining with the gestural loops of sand surrounding him; a woman in a bikini wringing out her wet hair, her head half-hidden beneath her long arms and fingers, her hips wide, her bottom and thighs loose and exaggerated; a woman lying on her side, leaning on one elbow, her back a curve, her head just a ball in her hand, her waist, legs and feet no more than a few billowy lines.

'These are really good,' I said.

I was resting my head on Clem's thigh, using it as a pillow, my bare shoulders nestled against his damp swimming shorts, my hair sticky and stringy from the salt water, a seaweedy smell in the air. Up ahead of us on the beach – a small, private-seeming one I hadn't known about in the Eastern suburbs, where Clem was confident we wouldn't bump into anyone from college – the sloppy greyish-green waves were flattening into bubbling white foam.

'You like them?' He sounded surprised. 'Just a bit of fun.'

'I do,' I said, flipping back through the pages of his drawing book, taking in the quickness and immediacy of his marks. He'd barely looked down at the paper while he'd been sketching or stopped to check if his lines were in the right places. Instead, he'd kept his eyes fixed on his subject, trusting that if he looked closely enough his hand would know exactly where to move. 'I like these ones a lot.'

There was a playfulness to Clem's sketches, a freedom and an inventiveness I'd never felt the presence of in his paintings. It made me wonder if shifting from a pencil to oil paint constricted him somehow; if the grand history of the brush – and his father's virtuosity with it – robbed Clem of something joyous, even choked his work.

'Your turn.' He passed me his pencil. 'I want a drawing of yours in my book. If it's any good, I'll tell people it's mine.'

I nudged his leg.

'Come on. One drawing. For me.'

I rolled onto my side, feeling cold but trying to ignore it. The day had been muggy and perfect for a swim, but the sky had turned overcast while we'd been out in the water and now the afternoon breeze was bringing a chill.

'I'm useless with charcoal,' I said. 'And that's good paper, you don't want to waste it.'

'Waste it. All of it, I don't care. So many rules you have, Frances.'

He was smiling at me, absently brushing charcoal off his hands, but I sensed something vaguely critical in his remark – an accusation of timidity, perhaps, or a frustrating lack of adventurousness. I'd felt troubled by the same sensation once or twice before in class, when he'd critiqued my work in front of the other students, calling it 'too careful' and 'predictable' and 'unoriginal' and 'tame' – all no doubt true, but still wholly crushing. At the time I'd passed it off as Clem making a show of treating me equally in front of the others, attempting to short-circuit any rumours about the two of us. (I was less worried about this possibility, since the notion of Clem and me being romantically involved must have seemed so inconceivable and ludicrous I was sure no one at college would ever believe it.)

I sat up, brought a corner of the towel over my legs, and flipped Clem's drawing book to a blank page. I brushed away the sand that had collected between the pages and looked around for something to draw. Eventually I settled on a low jagged rock formation on one side of the beach, with a boy in fluro shorts squatting near its edge like a bird considering flight.

Clem watched wordlessly over my shoulder as I moved the pencil around the page, using its smooth side more than its pointed tip. I could feel him following the unfamiliar logic of my marks, making sense of my choices. I didn't start with the boy – the figure – as I knew Clem would have. I started instead with the rocks – patches of deep black I blended out and reapplied charcoal to and blended out again, working the pigment into the paper with my fingers, rubbing it into a flat smoky wash of ocean and a hovering band of sky. For the boy, I drew an outline of his small body and then smudged it with my hand until he became more of an absence than a presence at the edge of the page.

'You're not into people much, are you?' Clem asked.

'I don't love drawing them, no.'

'But I mean in general. You don't like people. Being around them, talking to them. It makes you uncomfortable.'

I frowned and looked up at him, squinting in the last of the afternoon's glare.

'It's okay,' he said. 'I'm not having a go at you, Frances. I actually get it, I'm the same.'

'As what?'

'I don't connect with most people either.'

I tried not to laugh. Clem connected with everyone. He had more friends, more acquaintances, more fans, more sycophantic messages left on his answering machine (a lot of them by women) than any other person I'd ever known.

'Really, I don't,' he said seriously. 'Sure, I know heaps of people. And they all like to think they know me...' He looked at me, maybe waiting for me to say something, his eyes a little inflamed from the ocean. 'But they don't.'

He lifted his thumb and ran it gently over my bottom lip in a way I felt said, But you, Frances, *you* are the exception.

Then he moved it down my chin, my neck. Followed the round neckline of the one-piece swimsuit I still had from high school. Snuck it underneath the damp fabric and brushed it, feather-like, backwards and forwards over my nipple. I didn't know if anyone else was watching us. And I didn't care.

'Now I've distracted you.'

'Yes, you have.'

He moved his thumb away. Picked up the drawing book, still open to the page with my sketch.

'You should finish it. It was going somewhere.'

'No, it wasn't,' I said, wishing he hadn't stopped

touching me, wishing no one else was on the beach, my mind already rushing ahead to thoughts of us alone again in the haven of his studio.

'You're overthinking it,' Clem said. 'Just draw.'

'Maybe for you it's that easy.'

'No, it's difficult. Fucking painful most of the time. If I make one good drawing it's only because of the twenty other shit ones I made first. Same with paintings. But everything about being an artist should be hard or you're not pushing yourself. It's not all ability, it's about taking risks just as much, maybe more.'

'That's what you do, then? Just not think?'

Clem shrugged.

'I never know what I'm going to do before I do it. With a picture, or anything.' He lay down on the towel, crossed his arms behind his head, and closed his eyes. 'With me it's about getting lost in something – a figure, a face – and changing it. Transforming it into something that's completely mine, that's never existed before. Taking crazy liberties with it if I want. Making it weird and distorted to everyone else, who gives a fuck? But doing something only me and my marks could do to it.'

He opened his eyes for a second and looked at me, as if checking that I was still listening to him, still there. I touched his hand, my fingers hooking around his, and he closed his eyes again.

I remember thinking in that moment how, despite the intensity of our relationship – what felt like an insatiable need to be near each other, to be always touching – Clem still seemed like such a riddle to me. A disorientating, contradictory mix of confidence and self-doubt, openness and secrecy, intimacy and distance.

I lay down beside him and pressed my face against his chest.

'You're warm,' I said softly.

Clem brought his arm around my shoulder, letting me in closer.

'The important thing about a picture isn't to get it right, Frances. Fuck that. What you want to do is make it come alive.'

THREE

Suburban street, morning, oil on canvas, 40 × 50 cm

'Are you pregnant?'

I was sitting next to Albert at one end of a long dining table, digging into my meal of overcooked beef and soggy grey beans served on an antique Italian plate rimmed with gold. The hosts, Lydia and Theo, had just regaled everyone with the story of how they'd bought the plates the year before while on a quick trip to Venice for the Biennale, and also to celebrate their fifteenth wedding anniversary (which was a far longer stint, both joked, than either of their first or second marriages, which had been spectacular failures across the board). Not trusting the plates to the incompetence of the international postal service or the perils of the airline's cargo compartment, Lydia had delicately wrapped each one in pieces of her softest clothing – her cashmere pyjamas, silk camisoles, woollen scarves – and Theo had meticulously packed the twenty-piece dinner set into his carry-on case and nursed it like a baby the entire long-haul flight back to Sydney. Not a single plate had been so much as scratched, and to this everyone at the table had raised their glasses and wholeheartedly cheered.

Despite the way I was eating – barely stopping between mouthfuls, zoning out of the conversation to concentrate on loading my fork with the next bite – I wasn't enjoying the food. On the contrary, as the beans crumpled in my mouth and the beef resisted most of my attempts to cut it, I wondered how people so cultured and well-off could stuff up such a simple meal, and not seem remotely embarrassed (as I would have) serving it up to the high-powered guests sitting around the table. Lydia had cooked the dinner herself, which I gathered was unusual; the entire table had congratulated her for finding the time to boil beans and reheat corned beef she'd bought ready-made from a nearby deli on a hectic day of board meetings (Lydia chaired four).

I'd hardly eaten all day. Just a quick piece of toast for breakfast while Clem was still sleeping, and no lunch because I'd been on a roll painting down at the river and I didn't want to jinx things by stopping. The air was damp and silky after the rain the night before, the sunlight sticking to the mountains like a magnificent cobweb. I'd made about a dozen ink and gouache drawings from different angles – some with the river in the foreground, some of only the mountains and sky – and started a painting on board using a palette of yellows, greens and browns that felt like the beginning of something good.

I had spent so much of my time in Bald Hill lately sitting or assisting for Clem that I'd let my own work stall, and, while I kept this to myself, I was missing it. He was working to a pressing deadline for his next show with a top gallery in Melbourne and feeling anxious about it – 'in a funk', he admitted to me late one night when we were sitting together on the verandah, me wrapped in a blanket on his lap, his voice sounding flat and faintly ashamed after too much whisky. A review of his latest exhibition in a weekend paper had been vicious and humiliating, sending him into a resentful, depressed mood no amount of my attention or affection could shift. (I'd bought the paper from the general store and immediately hidden it in the bin after seeing the review, but he had searched for it and fished it out, and pored over every word.) For a week he refused to answer the phone – or to let me answer it – which rang incessantly. Even our sex that week became quick and mechanical; the more I tried to soothe him with it, the less interested he seemed.

The newspaper's longstanding art critic – who Clem said was a conservative dickhead and completely up himself, beyond his use-by date, a failed artist who still had a lot of sway – had labelled him 'a one-trick pony with the dubious (mis)fortune to have been sired by a thoroughbred', and mocked him as 'bucking and kicking for relevance as he stumbles towards the Big Four-O'. To worsen things, if that were possible, the paper had dug up an old photo of Clem from a magazine shoot ten years earlier that I sensed he regretted, of him sitting on a horse, wild-haired and shirtless, an air of Brontë's Heathcliff about him, wearing nothing but a pair of tight riding pants.

I hadn't gone more than a few days without painting or drawing for as long as I could remember. It had been my company, my comfort, my free ticket to elsewhere since I was a small girl staring out the window of a lonely, unfamiliar flat, my father gone, my mother undone, suspended somewhere out of reach like a lost balloon in the sky, shrinking away into the distance. But for the last month or so, whenever I'd seen my brushes and paints lying untouched on our shared work table, or walked past my paintings, half-started and drying out, pushed out of the way against the corrugated iron walls of the shed, I'd felt breathless.

I hadn't hesitated to say yes when Clem had asked if I would mind assisting him. He was getting stressed about his next show, he said, worried he'd run out of time to produce enough strong works. (And while he never exactly said so, never admitted it to me in words, I knew he wouldn't be able to cope with another bad review.) If I could spare some time to help him a little – stretch and prime his canvases, clean his palettes and brushes, lay in some of his backgrounds – it would make a huge difference. It was dull work, he knew, so he hated to ask. But if I wanted, I could also work on any fiddly patterns or intricate markmaking he might need. I had a light touch, he said. A discipline and containment his new works could probably use.

And while I loved the idea of helping Clem – of the two of us working side by side; collaborating, as I saw it – and was entirely flattered he had even asked, it was not the same as making paintings of my own. Which is why I had felt so relieved the morning of the dinner party to get back to it, back down to the river with my paints, spreading my sketches out on the grass as I finished each one; and why I'd forgotten all about going to Theo and Lydia's, and the three-hour drive it would take us to get there, until I opened the iron gate to the front yard and carried my work and equipment up the broken brick path to the tumbledown cottage Clem and I had been renting at that point for five months.

Clem was waiting on the wicker chair on the verandah, already dressed in a green velvet suit I didn't know he owned, a cigarette in one hand, his car keys in the other.

He was furious.

How could I have forgotten how important tonight was for him? He'd told me over and over. Invitations to dinner with the director of the Art Gallery of New South Wales might junk up his father's letterbox every second week, but for him this was a first. And really fucking important. What if Theo was thinking of acquiring one of his new works for the gallery's collection? Or curating him into a museum show? Or even offering him a solo one? Did I understand what it would mean for him to have his first non-commercial show and be recognised by a state gallery? Couldn't I at least have been ready to go on time? Or was I deliberately trying to fuck this up for him? Was that it? Was I jealous?

I'd never seen Clem so worked up or heard him sound so cold and incredulous. I tried not to feel like the student being scolded by the teacher and said I hadn't meant to upset him or mess up his night, and I'd be ready to leave in ten minutes.

'I'll wait in the car,' he said.

I stripped off my clothes and quickly washed my hands, face and armpits with soap in the bathroom sink, scrubbing off the paint and mud and sweat my skin had accumulated down at the river. It had been a glorious morning. I was still thinking about the filmy light and the gleaming greens reflecting off the water. The way it had felt as if the trees were calling to me, inviting me to watch the way they bent and shifted in the breeze. The way their leaves and branches stroked the river, like a lover.

I ran a brush through my hair, which had gone frizzy in the humidity, and dabbed some lipstick on my lips and cheeks with my fingers. I put on a pair of white lace underwear and Clem's favourite dress, the pink one with the shoulder ties he'd first painted me in. ('I'll never sell it,' he'd said of the portrait once he'd completed it and hung it up in his studio. 'I painted it for me.') It appeased him a little. Still, the drive to Theo and Lydia's harbourside home was mostly silent and tense, and took longer than it should have due to peak-hour traffic when we hit the city. My stomach was groaning but I didn't dare ask if we could stop for something to eat. Not even a packet of chips as we passed petrol station after petrol station, though I thought about it. When we were nearly there, Clem accelerated up the steep winding streets, as if our arriving ten or fifteen seconds earlier would make any difference.

We arrived forty-five minutes late but no one seemed to mind. Except maybe Clem, who went on about how terrible the city traffic had been, and how his poor old Mercedes was out of practice, having been parked on the dirt in the searing heat for months now at Bald Hill – a place that was less the inspiring artists' retreat he'd been led to believe, and more a ghost town in the middle of nowhere. The tin shed we had was impossible to paint in, like working in a fucking kiln. Not that there was anything there to paint. And we still had another month to go on the lease.

I suspected most of Clem's rant was intended for me. Renting a cheap cottage in Bald Hill, and painting and living there together for six months over the summer – Clem working on his next show, me developing a body of work that would hopefully earn me representation with a gallery and, in time, a debut exhibition – had been my idea. The town's gold-rush history and romantic decay had drawn me in, not to mention its remoteness from my flat and my suburb and my mother, all of which had begun to feel like dead skin I needed to shed. I'd asked Albert about Bald Hill, since he was the only artist I knew who had actually spent time there, and he told me of battered buildings that were once grand, of proud hard earth that had been ransacked and would eternally wear the wounds, of sweeping valleys and an emerald-green river that still sang with the voices of the long dead.

'For all its decrepitude,' Albert had told me, 'Bald Hill still holds a rich vein of gold. But the kind of gold known only to artists.'

The town had a legendary artistic lineage. In the forties, a coterie of Sydney's finest artists – later known as the Bald Hill Group – famously painted there, rendering its bleak streets and desolate buildings in rich ochres and dusty Venetian reds, producing works of rural decline and isolation that instantly became iconic. Generations of painters were inspired to follow, making artistic pilgrimages there in the fifties and sixties, reinterpreting the forms of the town's epic landscape with sensuous wheat yellows, golds and apricots. Even Albert had tried his hand there in the eighties, renting a small shack (since demolished) near the Candle River Track and painting a series of stirring portraits of the locals – old-time fossickers, rabbiters, recluses – their worn faces livid with strain in the aftermath of a devastating drought. Maybe, I had suggested to Clem, we could tap into Bald Hill's golden vein too.

Looking up, I realised I had stopped listening to Clem. No one else in the handsomely decorated sitting room was listening to him either. Not Hughie Chesterman, a longtime pal of Albert's and staunch collector of his work who, at seventy-nine, kept repeating how exhausted he was from his sellout performance as King Lear at the National Theatre in London ('Next time,' he said, 'someone remind me I'm too bloody old now for eight shows a week') and how excited he was to introduce his home town of Sydney to his new (fourth) wife, Zoe, who had stage-managed the production but couldn't face dinner because she was knocked over with jet lag.

Not Lydia and Theo, who were knee-deep in gossip about a well-known CEO accused of sexually assaulting a schoolgirl decades earlier, and who was currently facing court but had just donated two point five million dollars towards the gallery's refurbishment project – controversial in itself, since no one agreed on the design – which left a bad taste in the mouth, but no one was in a hurry to hand the money back. ('It's all so bloody long ago, who cares?' Hughie said, his huge belly hanging over the waist of his trousers, his paisley shirt stretched between the buttonholes and showing lumps of squashy white skin. 'The girl ought to thank him for the education.')

And certainly not Albert, who was sitting in a mustard-coloured armchair, saying little and looking sour, his legs crossed and arms folded, while his wife, Freya, who I'd never met before, tapped the carpet with the toe of a knee-high leather boot in time with the classical music playing on the stereo, and teased him about who might become the third Mrs Albert Hughes if he didn't stop sulking and cheer up.

'I realise we're boring you, darling,' Freya said. 'But you can't spend every night in your studio, much as you'd prefer it.'

No one paid attention to Clem and me. Or cared in the slightest that we were late. If anything, I got the impression it had been expected, even planned for. And not just because we'd had to drive so far to get there. As the conversation continued happily without us, I realised even Clem, who to me was so worldly and mature and urbane, was in their eyes still very much a child: unreliable, uninitiated, inconsequential.

The main course wasn't served until nine pm. Until then everyone was busy with the entrée, which was vodka any way you liked but mostly neat, prepared by Theo in the 'secret' bar under the stairs, a trip to which quickly revealed that his and Lydia's historic sandstone home was overcrowded with important pieces of twentieth-century Australian art. ('We have a real problem,' Lydia shamefacedly confessed to me when she took me on a tour of all three floors of the house. 'We keep buying paintings but we've run out of walls. I've had to stuff a Bill Dobell in there,' she said, pointing inside the kitchen pantry at a sombre painting of a horse and cart the size of a cereal box she told me she'd just bought for six figures at auction.) I asked for water please, which was met with a grunt and a grimace from Theo, as though I'd asked for a glass of poison. For the next hour I had to stop myself from eating all the olives and salted nuts in little hand-blown coloured glass bowls on the coffee table.

'I'm right, aren't I?' Albert said, when we were finally at the table with our meals. 'You're pregnant.'

It occurred to me Albert had been doing some adding up: I'd had water instead of vodka, I was eating a bad meal like a horse, and I'd been living with his son for five months in the middle of nowhere, the two of us with nothing to do besides paint and have sex, paint and have sex.

'No, Albert. I'm just hungry.'

He didn't look convinced. Perhaps a woman with an appetite and no good reason for it was inexplicable to him, unseemly somehow. Or maybe he was impatient for grandchildren, though I strongly doubted it. (I'd once heard him compare a toddler playing near his feet to an obstinate spaniel he'd once had.) Probably, I decided, Albert just enjoyed being right.

'The food's not wonderful,' he said, appearing not to care if Lydia or anyone else at the table heard him. He was on what I guessed was his fifth or sixth glass of red, not to mention all the vodkas, and had already spilled wine on the embroidered white tablecloth, where it had left an ugly blood-red stain that bulged all the way to my side plate. I imagined Lydia or Theo seeing it later on when they were clearing up – if they did their own clearing up – and assuming the mess was mine.

'I haven't eaten all day,' I explained to Albert, more apologetically than I felt like. 'I was painting.' In an effort to slow myself down, I rested my heavy silver cutlery on my plate and drank some more water.

'Good,' he said. 'Because it would be a mistake.'

'What would?'

'You. Having a baby.'

He took a mouthful of red wine and let it sit on his tongue a moment before swallowing. Then he leaned in close and grabbed my forearm. I could feel Freya watching us from across the table. She was seated between Clem and Theo but seemed uninterested in both of them, having pushed her chair back to allow the two men to talk across her, which they were doing, quite animatedly, Theo agreeing that the art critic who'd trashed Clem in the paper had zero understanding of any art made in the second half of the century, and was a smug old prick who did no one any favours. (One month earlier, Theo's blockbuster show of contemporary British artists, which had cost the gallery the earth in insurance, had been panned by the same critic, who described his viewing experience as 'about as pleasurable as a migraine'.)

I tried to ignore the feeling I had that Freya was assessing me, deciding if I was there to cause damage, or too simple to be capable; if I was a baby-faced harbinger of harm or just a naive young girl who was out of her depth and who would sink back into the wastelands where she belonged, far away from this table, soon enough. Freya was an independently wealthy widow with three children Albert had inherited. ('He only likes one of them,' Clem had told me in the car on the way there.)

'Name me one Australian female artist,' Albert began, unaware of – or deliberately ignoring – Freya's prickly stare, 'just one, who's had children and still been a success. Had a productive career. And I'm not talking Mary or June painting pictures of cows and carnations down at the local art show. I mean a serious artist. Who's won awards. Has pictures in the gallery.'

I went straight to my heroes. I thought of Clarice Beckett, pushing her painting cart up the wet and windy cliffs of Beaumaris, returning home after twilight, spooning soup into the mouths of her ailing parents, never marrying, never having children, dying young of pneumonia in both her lungs. I thought of Grace Cossington Smith, using her small square brushstrokes to paint iconic pictures of her sister knitting socks for soldiers and the Sydney Harbour Bridge before it was joined in the middle, living out her life in her parents' home in the quiet suburbs, dying in a nursing home, alone. I thought of Nora Heysen, the youngest and first female artist to win the Archibald Prize (and ridiculed for it by her male competitors), who wanted children but was unable to conceive. I thought of Jean Bellette, whose poetic and psychological works were wildly out of fashion, and whose wistful figures seemed to sigh with her strong belief that a serious artist should not have children. I thought of Margaret Olley, whose still lifes were printed on tea towels and umbrellas and fridge magnets you could buy in the gallery shop, who terminated her only pregnancy because she was convinced of the same.

But there was something else besides a child, it struck me in that moment, that most of the female painters I could think of had gone without. A different sort of demand on their time, a restriction on their freedom to paint, which they had consciously rejected or avoided: a husband. Could it perhaps have been this – an alternative kind of child, no less captivating and changeable and self-absorbed, no less in need of nourishment and attention – that had obscured or even obliterated countless female artists' work?

I thought again of Jean Bellette, whose paintings could not be mentioned by one of the most influential art critics of her time because she happened to be his wife. I thought of Stella Bowen, whose work as an official war artist I had studied at college, who famously neglected her art to nurture her womanising husband's, eventually having to leave him to carve out space for her own practice. I thought again of Nora Heysen, whose work fell into obscurity at the same time she became a wife, and who only resurrected her identity as an artist after her husband left her for a younger woman. There were so many similar, disillusioning stories. And they were by no means limited to Australian female painters. I thought of Lee Krasner and Celia Paul who, despite their talent, were better known as the long-suffering partners of art giants Jackson Pollock and Lucian Freud than as painters in their own right; two women artists mythologised as muses. And how many more were there? How many other female artists had been lost or, worse, never heard of?

'Can't think of one, can you?' said Albert. 'Because there aren't any.'

He was slurring. His mouth was sinking at the sides. His bottom lip had a crooked seam where the red wine had soaked and dried like blood. He was still holding onto my arm, his hand warm and a bit wet, as though he thought if he let go I might be at risk of running from the table into the path of an oncoming train.

'You have the heart of a painter, Frances. And I should know. I rarely see it, let alone say it. But it's one or the other, my dear. You can't have both. It's unfair, but you just can't. One will murder the other.'

There was no need for Albert to explain what he meant. Just as there had been no need for Clem to tell me he was only eight when his mother, Eva, had left him in their Paris apartment and never returned – though I'm sure he knew I'd heard the story. It was the art world's worst-kept secret that instead of walking to the market in the local square, as she did daily to buy bread and cheese and pastries for her husband and young son, Eva had walked in the opposite direction, to Pont Neuf, the city's oldest stone bridge. And though she couldn't swim and had always feared the water, Eva had removed her shoes and placed them neatly inside her straw bag, and jumped into the frigid green water of the river Seine.

Her body was not found for almost two weeks, held down by the river's powerful current in the murky depths with the creeping eels and the monstrous catfish and the city's sunken cars.

Albert had been so grief-stricken and unable to bear living in Eva's apartment – with her familiar smell still lingering on their bedsheets, and incomplete sculptures marked with her fingerprints everywhere he turned – that he'd fled Paris with his son and returned to Sydney. There, in a gloomy terrace, unwelcoming to visitors and silent with despair, Albert had drawn Clem over and over, not sending him to school, forcing the boy to instead sit for him every day for a year in an effort to feel closer to his lost wife.

The *Boy Clem* series, when it was finally exhibited at Porter Street Gallery as a suite of twelve paintings and three hundred and sixty-five works on paper – representing each month and day of the first year Albert had endured without Eva – had been both a critical and commercial disaster. Not a single painting sold, and barely any of the pencil drawings that had cost so much to frame made it out of the gallery. Collectors found the dingy palette and the boy's doleful look too miserable for their living rooms, and critics worried in writing that Albert's behaviour skirted uncomfortably close to abuse; that the grieving and sequestered young boy had been further wounded by his father's relentless artistic process. Nobody wanted to be part of it, or to be seen to condone it by having the work on their walls, however valuable it might one day become. In an unprecedented move Porter Street cancelled the exhibition, pulling down all the paintings and drawings after having displayed them for less than a week.

I had seen some of the *Boy Clem* drawings, ones that were never framed, stored in a steel map cabinet in Clem's studio when I first started visiting him there. Albert had given them to him, Clem said, as a coming of age gift on his eighteenth birthday. (He'd never known what to do with them, he'd told me. 'Who wants three hundred drawings of the darkest year in their life?') Carefully lifting them out one by one, I saw they were all drawn in coloured pencil on white Arches paper in soft pinks and browns. The lines were shockingly spare, and most of the paper left blank, so that in all of the drawings Clem looked empty, ethereal, as though he were disintegrating into air. Tracing my finger above their delicate surfaces, following

Albert's scant lines, I felt they were among his most tender and underrated works. The restrained colours, the economy and lightness of Albert's marks betraying the impossible weight of his emotions, the boyish innocence and unspoken loss in Clem's expression – all this had moved me. I'd felt pity for him, for both of them, and an unexpected protectiveness too.

Whenever we saw each other, Albert and I inevitably wound up talking about painting. We had little else in common, but on this topic all our differences vanished like pebbles in a mighty river. No other subject shot so directly to the core of our beings than the struggle to put paint on a canvas and turn it into truth. Ever since I'd graduated and Clem and I had gone public with our fledgling relationship, Albert had taken an unexpected interest in my career. At the time I thought, or hoped, he saw potential in my work. That he believed I had some genuine talent and a realistic future as an artist. Albert's attention felt like validation I wasn't wasting my time. His praise was as energising as the sun; he seemed capable of lifting day from night with a single nod and a few generous words. ('I like what you're doing here,' he'd said once, picking up a small painting I'd been working on of the street below Clem's studio. 'Letting your marks suggest but not explain.

There's a unique strength you have in withholding, Frances. A self-possession you must always try to keep.') But I wonder now if Albert simply enjoyed telling people how he thought they should be painting their pictures; how they should be living their lives.

Albert and I first spoke at my third-year graduation exhibition. He was there to support Clem, who had completed his one-year tenure as a guest tutor for the college. Enrolments had risen twenty per cent as a result and there was enormous pressure on Clem to stay for at least one more year. ('Too bad I have other plans,' he said to me at the end of a long sitting at his studio, after I'd raised the idea of us renting a place in Bald Hill. 'With you.' He smiled, his mouth travelling over the tiny mole below my nipple, inching into the shallow land between my breasts. I remember turning to look out the tall windows and the sun being too bright for my eyes, and closing them and feeling the warmth on my eyelids and thinking there was no part of me, no corner, no cell, that wasn't full.)

I was unaware of this at the time, but in the car on the way to the exhibition, Clem had told his father he'd been secretly dating one of his students for some months. Albert told me later he assumed the girl who'd taken Clem's fancy was Mimi. She had shaved half her head and was causing a stir (nearly as much as Clem's arrival with Albert had done) with her major work: a performance-art piece that involved her lying naked on a stainless-steel bench in front of a long mirror and painting a self-portrait on a white bedsheet using red ink and a meat cleaver. Clem had shaken his head, mouthed the word 'no' to Albert, and pointed to me.

I had been standing on my own near the back, beside my major work, away from the other students and their beaming dressed-up parents. (I hadn't mentioned the exhibition to my mother or invited her to come. She had always found my painting practice baffling and alien, and had never offered a word – good or bad – on my work, even when I was younger and still asked her to. My mother had scribbled phone numbers and shopping lists on most of the drawings I'd ever given her, so one day I stopped.)

I'd called my major work *Suburban street, morning* – hardly an original or imaginative title, especially compared to others on the wall that read like lines of quirky poetry – and, according to Clem, it was my strongest painting of the year. I had come to unthinkingly trust his opinion of my work, since I could never see straight when it came to judging my own paintings and I feared I sometimes confused the good with the bad. Clem had been so encouraging and supportive, inviting me to bring my work to his studio and use his expensive brushes and paints. He had more than enough space, he said, and I slept there half the time anyway. Plus, he was worried I'd asphyxiate myself if I kept working with oils in my tiny bedroom.

Clem had watched me work in his studio more closely than he'd ever done in class, and was constantly pushing me to take more risks, to start my paintings more quickly, to stop holding so tightly to their outcomes.

'Just hit it with a first mark,' he said, when I'd been lingering too long over a blank canvas. 'Don't worry if it's a mistake. It probably will be but it doesn't matter. You're going to make wrong decisions all over the place, Frances, but you can paint over them. That's the beauty of it. Nothing on a canvas is ever fixed. And if you really think you've fucked it up, just forget about it, throw it away and start another one.'

Clem had a way of making it all sound so simple and seductive. He was so casual about painting, even careless; always perfectly sure of himself and of what to do. And though I found it daunting, and it often left me feeling rudderless, I was influenced by everything he said and tried to absorb it into my own practice. Tried to loosen my style. Plan less, think less. Paint more quickly, more boldly, more intuitively. Be less deliberate with my marks.

And yet at the same time, I'd felt an equally strong pull in the opposite direction – something that sounded like my own voice quietly pushing back, telling me to be patient, to take my time and search for the truth of every detail, to not lose my way of treading gently, watchfully, of revealing an image rather than imposing one, of allowing the painting to do most of the work itself.

But the more I now stared at my major work, the more fault I found, the more glaring mistakes I saw, and the more ashamed I felt to have it hanging on the wall in front of so many people. I wasn't sure anymore why I had let Clem convince me to put it in the show when I could see now it was nothing more than a sloppy, confused landscape, with no feeling in the marks, and not even painted particularly well.

And to make things a thousand times worse, Albert Hughes was walking over in his tweed sports jacket and beige trousers.

He stood right beside me and we exchanged a nod but no words – even though he now knew who I was, and I needed no one to inform me who he was. Then, for a number of excruciating minutes, he stared at my painting.

Albert's arms were folded across his chest and his lips were pressed together in concentration. I tried not to look at him – at least not obviously – but my eyes kept veering sideways. I was desperate but terrified to know what he was thinking. Despite the noisy chit-chat in the room all I could hear was the sound of Albert breathing.

He took a step towards my painting, moving close enough to scrutinise the surface and the brushstrokes.

Close enough to see where my gestures had been indecisive, where I'd had second thoughts or made errors and tried to bandage them up. I could feel him dissecting my picture as keenly as a surgeon armed with a tray of sharp silver instruments; dissecting my internal organs, dropping them into glass jars of formaldehyde, holding them up to the light to inspect their weaknesses and imperfections.

I wanted to hide. For a moment I considered sneaking out the door and jumping on the first bus home, resolving never to be deluded enough to pick up a paintbrush again. But it was hopeless. Impossible now to disconnect myself from the painting on the wall in front of us. I wondered if I could pretend the student name and photograph (a horrible one – I looked bug-eyed and stunned) on the information card beside it weren't mine. I had worked the painting too hard, I saw now. Wrestled with it for too long. Overplayed my strokes. I'd spent weeks on it; the composition had not come easily, so I kept scraping it back, starting again and again, leaving the ghosts of my failed attempts to haunt the canvas. I never knew when to put down my brush. When to walk away from a painting and accept it was done. Instead, I would doggedly stick to it, argue with it, try to fight it into shape. And now, standing beside one of the country's most luminary painters, I would have to take responsibility for the strangled result.

'You've caught something here,' Albert said.

He looked at me over the top of his round tortoiseshell glasses.

'Sorry?'

'The peculiar emptiness of the suburbs – well, that goes without saying: the dowdy brick house, the empty street, the telegraph pole interrupting the foreground. Those are almost tropes. And nothing plenty of other artists haven't already done before you, and better.'

He uncrossed his arms and used his middle finger to push his glasses up the bridge of his nose. I saw that his nails were neatly clipped. Then he sniffed, slid both hands into his trouser pockets, and took another step towards the painting. He almost had his nose to it.

'But the pallid colours are a surprise,' he said. 'So quiet and subdued they shouldn't work, but they do. They almost glow. You've painted the sky as if it's water.' He looked at me again, our eyes connecting, I felt, for the first time. 'It has the slippery feeling of a dream. All in soft focus. Something you can only half remember, can't quite see the detail of anymore, but can still sense.' He nodded slowly, more to himself than to me. 'It's well done.'

For a few seconds I didn't know what to say, unsure if he was being serious or just kind. Probably, I thought, he felt obliged to compliment all his son's students.

'Thank you,' I said politely. 'That's very nice of you to say.'

'I'm not nice. Ask anyone. And I don't say things I don't mean. It's a strong little picture. There's a depth of feeling in it. An unlikely intensity. And grace.'

I felt my face flood with surprise and I broke into a smile. And while I tried to immediately contain it – determined not to embarrass myself by looking foolish and overwhelmed – I'm sure Albert saw it meant a great deal to me that he liked my work.

'I lived in that house, on that street, in that suburb,' I said. 'And I promise you it was anything but graceful.'

Albert nodded again and said, 'I'm sure you're right. Painting is illusory, after all. We keep and discard details as we need. Transpose them. Invent new ones if it suits us better. We're believers in art, not fidelity. There are no rules. But that's not what you're telling me here.' He gestured at the sallow low-hanging sky. 'And here.' At the nebulous lilac shape on the left that was my childhood home. 'And here.' At the silver asphalt of the street, barely perceptible as it receded into darkened space. 'To me, this painting reads like a love letter.'

I stood there holding my arms and wanting to tell him how wrong he was. How little love I had for the first place where I had lived. All those long hours alone in my bedroom, staring out my window at our driveway, no birds or movement in the sky, the neighbours' houses hemmed in so tightly I could hear them flushing their toilets, feeding their dogs, smacking their children. And late at night, down the dark hallway, my parents fighting on the good white carpet, unaware I was awake and could hear them, or beyond caring. My first home in the suburbs felt entirely disconnected from me now. A detail from my past that might eventually be painted over and not matter.

'For a painting of a street, it's surprisingly humane,' Albert said. 'And more intriguing the longer you look at it. You should enter it in a competition. Any of them. You might win.'

There was an air of authority to everything Albert said. A conviction and certainty that made me almost believe him.

'I think I've got a long way to go before that.'

'A pleasant sign you're not a narcissist. Unlike our poor friend over there.'

He was looking at Mimi, who had spilled her red ink and accidentally rolled in it, and was now mopping it off her stomach and backside.

'What a mess,' Albert said, not quietly. I was fairly sure he wasn't talking about the ink.

'When a painting works,' he said, meeting my eyes, his voice soft and almost secretive, 'it's a revelation. More to the artist than to anyone. The best paintings have minds of their own. They fall into our hands, fully formed, and our only job is to be ready to receive them and put them on the canvas. They paint themselves,' he said, his blue eyes sparkling, 'and catch us up later.'

I'd painted the house from memory, which was unusual for me. Normally I painted from life; en plein air, as Albert liked to say, with his impressive French accent. At the very least, I made my pencil or ink sketches outside – dozens and dozens of them in drawing books I kept in my satchel or, when I could afford it, on Arches paper that I folded neatly and tore up into smaller squares to make the paper go further. I would carry them all back to my bedroom or Clem's studio, where I would lay out the best ones on the floor to use as references for paintings. But even at the time of the graduation exhibition, I think I sensed that if I were to go back to my first home, all I'd see would be an ordinary two-storey house at the end of a treeless street, forgettable in a sea of identical houses butting up against it on all sides.

In my memory, though, our house was singular. Colossal. A universe of blond bricks, red roof tiles and white wrought-iron railings that formed the landscape of my childhood, such as it was.

I was small, about four years old I think, the first time I woke in the dark to the sound of my parents arguing about selling our house. Even at that young age, I understood what that meant. Knew instinctively what the cocky red and white *For Sale* sign pegged into our front lawn intended to steal from me. I had crept from my room into the shadowy hallway often enough late at night and caught sight of my parents wrestling in the sunken lounge room, rolling around and around like dogs, slapping and scratching at each other's half-demented faces, to know that our family was ending.

My bedroom was at the front of the house and everything I remember being in it was yellow: yellow bed and bedspread, a set of wooden drawers painted yellow, yellow daisy curtains, yellow rocking chair, yellow toy box, even a fluffy yellow beanbag in the shape of Big Bird from Sesame Street, with orange legs that I folded around myself when I sat on him.

The room had a square window that overlooked the front lawn and some of the concrete driveway that led to our garage. If I stood on my toy box, my eyes could reach above the windowsill and I'd have a good view of whoever was coming or going. From there, I had seen my father throw our plastic green tree out the front door on Christmas Eve, the smashed fairy lights and broken glass decorations twinkling like a miniature galaxy of coloured stars on the driveway under the streetlight. 'Fuck Christmas!' my father yelled from his car to any of the neighbours who might have been watching, daring them to have a problem with it, his tyres squealing as he accelerated away.

My father had a habit of throwing things. I had seen him hurl a rock the size of a human head through the rear window of my mother's car, the glass shattering and leaving a gaping hole that, from my bedroom, seemed like a giant black eye, watching us darkly. My father had gone to throw it at the bonnet first, intending, I guess, to smash the engine and do more significant damage. But my mother had spread her body across the bonnet, her arms and legs outstretched as if she were making a snow angel, to stop him. My mother loved her car.

One day a family named the Lansers (I've never forgotten their name) came with a suited real estate agent to inspect our house. I watched the mum (pointy-faced) and the dad (moustached) and the two kids (boys, tall, both in Star Wars t-shirts) walk across the good white carpet in the lounge room without taking off their shoes, which, as I understood things, was equivalent to a crime. My mother had whacked me across the legs with the thin plastic end of the feather duster as punishment for doing precisely the same thing in my school shoes, and I'd been startled by how quickly my pale skin swelled up into angry crosshatched red lines. But now I watched in bewilderment as my mother stood there and smiled benignly while the Lansers trampled around our lounge room in their dirty shoes. I stood at the front door and watched them leave, then asked my mother why she had let them do it.

'This house is for a family,' she said, not looking at me, staring absently into the street. 'We're something else.'

I found the axe in a corner of the garage, leaning against the back wall with the shovel and the rake. It was heavier than I expected and nearly as tall as I was; I had to reconsider my plan of carrying it down the driveway to the front lawn and resorted to dragging it there instead. Lifting and swinging it proved even more problematic, and the first couple of times I missed the wooden post of the *For Sale* sign altogether, the weight of the axe tipping and spinning me in circles as if we were partners in some frenetic dance, until I dropped it and collapsed onto the grass.

I don't remember worrying that my parents or one of the neighbours might catch me in my act of vandalism and try to stop me. I felt curiously invisible, outside the realm of everybody else, as though they'd all been put to sleep by some magical and beneficent spirit, like in one of the fairy tales I read to myself at night, so that I could see my clever idea through to fruition. If there was no *For Sale* sign, I figured, there could be no sale, and if there was no sale we would not have to move out, and the Lansers would not be able to move in, and my family, unpredictable and turbulent as it was, would stay together. Chopping down the sign, I believed, would fix everything.

I picked up the axe and swung again.

'Albie said something about you having a show?'

Freya was sitting on the arm of a chesterfield sofa, fiddling with her rings, twisting them around her long fingers. Her fingernails were painted red but one was chipped and looked as though a rodent had nibbled on it.

'No,' I said. 'I don't even have a gallery yet.'

'You're being modest. Albie wouldn't make it up.'

Freya's habit of calling him 'Albie' annoyed me. It didn't suit him; it sounded cutesy and childish. No one ever abbreviated Albert's name; something about it – something about him – demanded a certain fullness and formality. But perhaps Freya knew this, and it was precisely why she did it.

'I've got two paintings in a group show,' I said. 'That's probably what he meant. But it's hardly the same thing. I don't know why he mentioned it.'

'Albie rates your work,' Freya said plainly. 'He's told me so, several times. Anyone would think he likes it better than Clem's, the way he goes on.'

Freya's fine straight hair was the colour of pale straw and her eyes were unlike any I'd ever seen: crisp, blue and bewitching, like the sky at high altitude, too icy to be habitable. I could see why Albert liked painting her. She was unearthly.

'Clem wants it so badly,' Freya said. 'To know he's gifted. The real thing. Not just a weak forgery of his father.'

She was looking outside, beyond the french doors into the pretty courtyard where Clem was smoking cigars with Albert, Theo and Hughie under the canopy of a gnarled wisteria vine, his green velvet suit catching the light, gleaming like fur. Clem was clearly drunk, throwing his head back and swaying on his feet, laughing too loudly and for too long, probably at his own jokes.

'Doesn't take a genius to see he's wanted it his whole life,' Freya said. 'But what if you're the one who's got it?'

She was staring at me with her strange cold eyes.

'Might be why he's attracted to you, in some screwed up masochistic way. As well as the obvious, of course. Clem has wonderful taste. Only ever goes for the attractive ones.'

Freya stood up from the sofa and walked across the room to a small painting on the wall right beside me, of a sunny seaside village in the south of France. It was a Stella Bowen, painted on board, probably around the twenties, still in what looked like its original wooden frame.

'I'm no painter. Can't even draw a stick figure, so what would I know?' Freya said. 'But do you think there's room in one relationship for two ambitious artists?'

I felt my jaw tighten and my cheeks flush red. I didn't like talking about my work at the best of times, but especially not here in the sumptuous home of the man who ran the state gallery, and not pitted against Clem.

Or maybe it was Freya I didn't like. Everything about her felt cunning and dangerous, like a distant bushfire tossing up embers that could land at your feet.

'He'll tire of you, either way,' she said flatly. 'He always does.' Then she smiled at me almost coyly, touching my shoulder. 'So, where's the group show? I'd love to see it.'

'Baumann's,' I said, pretending I hadn't heard her. Pretending her words weren't repeating in my mind: He'll tire of you. He always does.

I'd never wanted to ask Clem about any of the girlfriends he'd had before me, though I knew there must have been a few. I'd seen photographs – some old, some not so old – floating around his studio of him with other women. And there were all the paintings and drawings of other women too. But it was impossible to know if they had been his lovers or friends or just models – Clem was so tactile with everyone and naturally flirtatious. A photo of him kissing a woman could just as easily have been him with a girlfriend as him with someone he'd met five minutes ago at an opening. Still, I compared myself to all of them negatively – not as pretty, not as voluptuous, not as fashionable, not as cool.

'Oh, you're showing with Tobias,' Freya said.

I couldn't tell if she was impressed or amused; it seemed like both.

'Just for this one group show.'

'I doubt it. He'll want to sign you up in a flash, particularly if you sell. Tobias knows where his bread's buttered.'

'We haven't talked about it.'

'Not the best space he's got. Too small, makes me claustrophobic. But the location's perfect.'

She returned to the arm of the sofa and crossed her legs. Her pointy leather boots shone.

'Tell me, has he hit on you yet?'

'No,' I said, having anticipated her question. Tobias had a reputation, and whether or not he had made a pass at me seemed the first thing anybody wanted to know. 'I'm not his type.'

'Oh, but you are.' Freya laughed. 'You tick every box, Frances. You're an artist, you're young, female, gorgeous, talented. You're bang on his type.'

If I'd had any nerve – which I didn't – I would have argued with her. I felt like arguing with her. But I knew I would lose. Tobias Baumann was a sleaze, or so everyone kept telling me. Rumour had it he'd told a young Sylvia Nickels she'd 'blown it' when she arrived at her debut opening at Baumann's on the arm of a retired banker and flashing a diamond ring on her engagement finger. Realising he'd have no chance with her, Tobias had immediately dropped Sylvia from his stable of artists, or badmouthed her to every other art dealer in the city so no one would touch her, or refused to pay her for her paintings, even the ones he'd already sold; the story took different turns depending on who told it. But whatever had gone wrong between them, it was Tobias who had ultimately blown it – and a fortune in commissions – since Sylvia Nickels had gone on to win every lucrative painting prize in the country, and to exhibit, among other places, at the Saatchi Gallery in London.

I didn't want to admit it to Freya, but Baumann's was not my first choice of gallery. It had none of the history or prestige of a place like Porter Street, and lacked the daring ambition of a young contemporary space. Showing at Baumann's was a lot like living in the suburbs – somewhere between the sparkle of the city and the solidity of the country. I felt comfortable there, if not overly inspired. And I reassured myself that every artist had to start somewhere.

Tobias lived by the mantra that paintings always sold better in gold frames, and while this was not my style – I preferred simple timber ones, if I chose to frame my work at all – his well-heeled clients appeared to agree, buying paintings from him by the truckload. Despite his dubious reputation and mediocre gallery space, Tobias could not only sell out shows but could also kickstart careers, matchmaking artists with collectors who would stick with them for life. And no one, it seemed, not even those on Tobias's long list of detractors, denied he had a good eye.

'Why so pale?' was the first thing Tobias asked me at the lunch meeting I'd secured with him less than a month after my graduation, by mailing his gallery ten high-quality photographs of my work. (I had done the same thing with seven other galleries in the city, but Tobias was the only dealer to reply and to return my photographs. 'These would have cost you a lot,' he'd said.)

At the time, I was happy to believe Tobias had responded genuinely to my work, seeing something fresh in it, perhaps, something youthful that might have appealed to some of his clients. But over the years I've sometimes wondered if Tobias had heard I was dating Clem Hughes, and if it was this particular detail, more than any spark of brilliance he may have seen in my paintings, that caught his attention. I'll never know, and too much time has passed now for me to ever ask him.

'They're verging on too soft to see,' Tobias said. 'Which for some buyers could be a problem.'

He'd brought my envelope of photos with him and was spreading them out on the table with his broad quick hands, like a croupier at a casino.

'But they've got presence, that's for sure. They're mysterious. I like that.'

Tobias had made a point of telling me as we sat down that he was paying for the meal and to order whatever I liked. I was tempted to get the eye fillet I saw being delivered to a nearby table – the gleaming steak standing in an elegant round, four centimetres tall, dripping with Café de Paris butter and half-buried in frites. But when the waiter came to our table and took a pencil from behind his ear and stared down at me, I ordered the same dish as Tobias: a beetroot and walnut salad with buffalo mozzarella and figs.

'I've always painted with a muted palette,' I said, once the waiter had moved on. 'I don't know why. There's no great reason. Just the way I see things, I guess.'

Tobias sipped on his wine.

I watched him nervously, worried he was unsatisfied with my answer. I was unsatisfied with it too. But the right words never came to me in the right moments – especially about my work – which is why I had always found it better to keep my thoughts to myself. You were never in danger of saying the wrong thing if you said nothing.

'That won't do for the catalogue,' Tobias said. 'Buyers want to know why you've made certain choices. Why you paint the way you do. So they can sound intelligent when your work's up on their wall and someone asks what it's about, and why they paid so much money for it.' He refilled my glass, which I'd barely touched, and then his own with the expensive pinot gris he'd ordered. 'No one wants to look stupid. Definitely not art collectors.'

Tobias's solid square face was pockmarked, the skin on his forehead and cheeks a constellation of pitted scars. He'd suffered badly from acne in his past, there was no hiding it. But in a peculiar way this only added to his appeal, the crater-like marks giving him the battle-scarred look of a warrior, of someone who'd fought tenaciously to be where he was. I identified with this somehow, and so, despite all the shady rumours about him, I felt oddly safe; Tobias was an outsider too.

'I couldn't tell you how many times someone's stood in front of a painting at one of our openings and said, "I could do that. I could paint that in my sleep. My two-year-old could do a better job." Kid you not, I hear it all the time. And not just from the freeloaders only there for the alcohol. These are people with money. And brains.'

He picked up a dinner roll from the basket and started ripping it apart, dipping each piece into a little dish of olive oil and balsamic vinegar, chewing while he talked.

'Just last week, this collector walks in. Serious guy, knows his stuff, super wealthy family, good client, the guy's bought from me for years. Says he wants to look at some Lucy Ming paintings. So I say brilliant, I sit him down, give him a glass of wine and pull out this incredible piece. Two metres long, a diptych. She used eighty kilos of paint. *Eighty*. Takes two people to lift the thing. It's a monster.'

I knew Lucy Ming's work. It was abstract, textural, heroic; dense, hulking paintings in thick layers of seductive high-pitched colour that transcended identifiable forms. One had recently sold to the National Gallery for a quarter of a million dollars.

'Know what he said, this guy? After sitting there looking at it in dead silence for ten minutes?'

'Too heavy?' I said.

Tobias laughed and pointed a finger at me. 'You've got a sense of humour. I like that. Not enough artists do. Take themselves too seriously.'

I wasn't trying to be funny. Eighty kilos sounded like a lot of weight for one wall. But maybe it wasn't?

'He said a monkey could have painted it.'

'Wow,' I said. 'That's so rude.'

'Maybe.' Tobias shrugged. 'Or maybe it's just the kind of ignorant thing people say when they feel locked out of a picture. When they don't know what it's about or what they should be thinking. When it makes them feel inadequate. And who wants to buy a big piece of that and take it home, put it up on their wall for everyone to see?'

The waiter arrived with our identical meals and placed them on the table as Tobias kept talking, the two of them exchanging small nods. I got the feeling Tobias ate here a lot.

'Of course it can work the other way round too. People can go out of their way to buy something they don't understand because they think other people will, people more in the know, and it'll make them look smarter. Or other people *won't* get it, and that'll still make them look smarter, not to mention audacious as well. There's so many reasons I could tell you why people do and don't buy a painting. Being a dealer's more like being a counsellor half the time. You find out a lot. Why do you think I put a sofa in the gallery?'

He raised a knowing eyebrow as he pushed a chunk of fig into his mouth with his thick fingers and drank it down with a sip of wine.

'Point is, I think your paintings are good, Frances. Could be really good, who knows? I've got that feeling. But they're difficult. Not easy to read. They hide as much as they reveal. Which is heading into risky territory.'

He did the thing with his eyebrow again and I found myself nodding. I wasn't even sure why, or what I was agreeing with, but it seemed important.

'Don't get me wrong, I'm not saying you should dumb down your paintings. I like that they're enigmatic, that's their power. But they need a story. A key to let people in. Doesn't matter what it is, only matters that you've got one.'

He picked up his fork and waved it distractedly as he went on talking.

'So, are you into these bleached colours because you're playing with a feeling of nostalgia? Déjà vu? Because that could work. Or maybe your paintings look all soft and serene but they're actually ironic, hard-edged, and it's your very sharp, critical way of looking at the world kind of flipped, through this hazy lens? That could work too. Or,' he said, shrugging and stabbing his last piece of beetroot, 'it could be dead simple and you're just a romantic. You see beauty in places where other people don't.'

I hated the walnuts. They were coated in so much sugar they kept sticking to my back teeth, and I had to curl my tongue sideways to try to unstick them. On so many levels, I regretted not ordering the steak.

I looked up and realised Tobias had stopped talking and was waiting for me to say something. I wiped my mouth with my napkin.

'I don't know why I paint the way I do. Or how to explain it. If I could do that, I probably wouldn't need to paint it.'

Tobias looked at me a long moment, as if sizing me up. I felt sure I had made no sense, that I had underwhelmed him, and ruined any chance I might have had of showing with his gallery by being so vague and disagreeable.

'Know what they say about artists?' he said, lifting the bottle of pinot gris from its silver ice bucket and emptying what was left of it into my glass. 'Besides the fact they're a moody, unreliable bunch who could all use some therapy?'

'No.'

'Whatever they paint, they're always painting themselves. Doesn't matter if it's a bridge or a bunch of flowers or a teapot. Could be nothing but abstract colour – it's still always them.'

By the end of lunch I had agreed to a thirty–seventy split the gallery's way, Tobias making it clear that as an unknown artist two seconds out of art school I had no bargaining power whatsoever; that the exposure I'd get from having two paintings in a group show for emerging artists at Baumann's at this early point in my career was priceless; and that thirty per cent was better than twenty, which was what he'd planned to offer me, except he liked me and thought I had promise.

When I relayed all this to Clem later – in his car on our way to Bald Hill for the very first time – he shook his head and told me I'd been played. That Tobias would have expected me to haggle for sure – why hadn't I? That no artist in their right mind – even a naive and nameless one like me – agreed to only thirty per cent. That Tobias was a shark.

But the thought of haggling had never crossed my mind. I was in my first show at a proper commercial gallery. I was done with art school and now officially about to exhibit. If I was lucky, my paintings might even sell.

I had left home, and my mother, and the dim suburb where I'd been stuck for twenty years. I was in my pink dress in the passenger seat of Clem's old cream Mercedes, speeding up the highway at a hundred and ten kilometres an hour, the windows down and the hot summer wind whipping my face, my bag of clothes and satchel of art materials behind me on the back seat; on my way to a distant town perched high in the mountains, close to the sky, that I'd only seen in paintings and read about in art books, where I was going to live and work with Clem, the man I adored and who, improbably, adored me too, the two of us creating art together that would make our names.

I was happy.

FOUR

Clem, asleep (unfinished), ink on paper, 37 × 54 cm

Clem was still sleeping when I slipped out of bed. His breathing was heavy, punctuated by snores that caught abruptly in his throat before they had time to fully expand; a familiar sign he'd drunk too much red wine. Which was no surprise, as I'd drunk too much with him.

The cottage was silent and dark as I crept naked from the bedroom towards the front door. The pads of my toes slid into the gaps between the wide floorboards where the cool night air wafted up from the darkness below. I'd always meant for us to buy a few rugs – soft Persian ones in clay pinks and vermillion reds, like those I'd seen in the windows of the dusty second-hand shops we drove past when we were down the mountain to buy our weekly groceries. (The Bald Hill General Store could be relied on for milk, yesterday's white bread, yesterday's newspaper and anything that could be preserved for years in a tin; but fresh fruit and vegetables, and any kind of meat that wasn't roadkill, required a one hundred and forty kilometre round trip down the winding gravel road into town.) But it was too late now. I'd run out of time. At the end of the week our lease was up, and Clem had already packed his car to leave.

The landlord had offered us longer.

'Another three months if you'd like. Or more. And if it's an issue, darling, we can look at the rent. Nothing's set in stone.'

Euan was in his late sixties, an old-school gentleman with silky pearl-coloured hair. He was an antique jeweller with a small workshop and an art-deco flat above it on King Street in Sydney. His partner, Matteo, ran a popular bistro around the corner with dark bentwood chairs, little round tables draped with white tablecloths, a bar stacked with imported wines from Tuscany and Bordeaux, and the daily menu written across a brass mirror that hung above a long wooden counter. (I would eat there often over the years whenever I was in Sydney, almost always at the same table by the front window overlooking Hyde Park, and while I always tried to pay, Matteo would never accept a cent from me, waving my money away as if it might bite him, putting a hand to my face and saying, 'We's family, bella.')

Euan and Matteo had bought the Bald Hill cottage together on a whim in the eighties, when they were tiring of their social scene in Sydney and thought to buy a cheap place with old bones in the mountains, and do it up as their own private getaway. But the cottage required far more work than either of them had anticipated, and they'd had to do most of the renovations themselves since there were so few qualified tradesmen in Bald Hill to help, and the six-hour round trip to Sydney soon proved too exhausting to manage in one weekend; not to mention the constant difficulty of finding dependable staff to manage the bistro while Matteo was away, and the fact that long hours in the car caused Euan's sciatica to flare. As a result, the cottage had stood empty for months, even years, at a time.

'It's worth a lot to me just knowing there's someone there, looking after the place. Making sure it doesn't go to rack and ruin,' Euan had said the day before, when I'd called to ask him where he'd like me to leave the keys when we left. 'I feel dreadful thinking of it just sitting there, empty and closed up again, no one enjoying it, when it's such a special place. Not everybody sees that about Bald Hill, I know. All they see is the neglect and the mess. The hard weather. The dryness. Everything that doesn't work and isn't there.' He laughed in his polite hooting way. 'Boy, do I hear enough of that from Matteo. How there's nowhere to get a decent espresso, even if you drive an hour down the mountain. But you're an artist, Frances, and you see it, don't you? I can hear it in your voice, darling. You've fallen in love with the place too.'

Euan wasn't wrong. The last thing I wanted to do was leave Bald Hill. I had seen myself, in some dreamy corner of my mind I rarely allowed myself to visit, living in that ramshackle cottage and painting the vast landscape surrounding it forever. I knew I would never tire of it. Felt sure I would be able to look at the same mountain or sky or river or tree I'd painted fifty or even a hundred times before, and still find something new in it. Something unseen. A concealed colour or unexplored shape. A twist of a branch I hadn't noticed.

'If money's tight, you could pay me in paintings,' Euan had said. 'Yes, there's an idea, pay me with your art instead. I'd like that better, to tell you the truth. Money's so crude, and I have more of it than one geriatric queer will ever need. But a painting by you, darling, of the cottage, or a sunset over Bald Hill, that I could hang here in my workshop and look at every day – now that would be special.'

Euan had seen my two works at the group show at Baumann's. As it happened, he was one of Tobias's clients, irregularly buying small pieces of art for his and Matteo's flat. He had an eclectic collection that followed no rules or trends and was slim on big names. Euan had never purchased art with the intention of selling it on the secondary market to make a profit; he simply bought what he liked, the pictures he wanted to live with, the paintings that spoke to him.

'Haunting little things,' Euan had said of my two suburban landscapes. 'Forlorn and pulsing with unease. But so gorgeous and gentle with the colours. I just loved them. Alas, I was too slow, both already had red dots.'

I earned my first money from selling paintings in that show at Baumann's. Tobias had promptly sent me a cheque for my thirty per cent – a total of three hundred dollars – with a handwritten letter on his personalised stationery saying he could have sold each painting ten times over, his clients had responded to them in a big way, and some were pretty upset they'd missed out, so would I like to join his stable and have a solo show at the end of the year? We could discuss the terms over lunch – same place, his shout – when I was back in Sydney. He was open to negotiating his commission and obviously my prices had to be reconsidered. And we'd need to decide how often I should exhibit. Once a year would be ideal if I could manage it, but every eighteen months would also work. And we should talk about competitions – I needed to start entering them and getting my name out there, expand my audience. I was a contender, he thought, to hang in the Wynne Prize. But there were other prizes too – international ones for landscapes – with better prize money and bigger exposure. The important thing was he saw a long and bright future ahead for us, and if I said yes he'd be delighted to represent me.

Clem told me to ignore him. To cash the cheque as soon as possible in case it bounced, but to throw his letter – and his offer with it – in the bin. Tobias and his gallery were second-rate. I could do better than tying myself to a big-talking dealer with nothing to offer but a shitty little space. Perceptions mattered in the art world, more than I knew, and I might never recover from a poor first move, no matter how strong my work was. I should wait, Clem said, like he'd told me to – what was the point of him giving me advice if I didn't take it? I needed to get a serious body of work together first. Spend a year on it, two if I had to, and aim for a gallery that counted. He and Albert could help me get my foot in the door anywhere. But – was I listening to him? – Tobias was a mistake.

That's how our argument had begun – over Tobias. I had listened to everyone's warnings about who and what he was, how sleazy and greedy and ingratiating he could be, and how I would never be able to trust him. But I had seen no evidence of those things myself. Tobias was a salesman, yes; he'd never tried to deny it. He was a man who did everything – talk, eat, make deals – in a hurry, as though his time were always in danger of running out. But I also felt Tobias was someone who genuinely understood my work – in a way that, at the time, I wasn't sure I understood it myself. Someone who could help me find the right words for it, when words were necessary. And not least, Tobias knew how to get my paintings onto people's walls. Perhaps not the right people's walls, according to Clem, not the walls of important wealthy collectors. But Tobias already had a waiting list of clients who were interested in buying whatever I painted next. This was something I knew Clem could never really understand, and that I was only brave enough to say to him when I was drunk: that I had no famous father or whopping inheritance to rely on like he could. That while I was grateful for his offer, I could think of nothing worse than him or Albert pushing my foot in any doors – for me, that was not how it worked. ('How the fuck else does it work?' Clem had said.) If I didn't take Tobias's offer there were no guarantees I would ever get another, let alone one with a gallery better than Baumann's; certainly no other dealers had called, despite a favourable (and thrilling) two-line mention of my work in the weekend paper. (The critic, a woman Clem had never heard of, described my style as 'hushed and entrancing' and said I was 'one to watch'.) There was no room for me to take chances, or experiment, or take a year or two to find my artistic language, as Clem had been free to do. I would have to work for the privilege of being an artist. I would have to earn my moments of immersion in my work.

But perhaps Clem and I had started arguing months earlier, possibly even on our first drive up to Bald Hill. We had been stretching apart, little by little, like the sun lifting away from the horizon at dawn – only I hadn't acknowledged it, or hadn't wanted to; the idea of us not working, not being together, was, to me, unthinkable. I had grown so accustomed to Clem's contrariness and fickle moods. Learned to read his face like the weather, and know when our day would be sunny and fine or, increasingly, dark. His tense look if I lifted a brush to work on a painting of my own instead of one of his. His silence when I talked about entering my work in competitions, as Albert and Tobias had both suggested. The way he'd avoid my eyes and light a cigarette, or blast some music, or talk on the phone to one of his many friends I didn't know, or sit up drinking whisky on the verandah alone instead of coming to bed with me. The way he'd kicked over his easel and yelled how everything was fucked, this shithole place I'd dragged him to was fucked, there was nothing here to paint. How he began turning his body the other way the moment we'd finished having sex. The strange ambivalence I began to feel from him; the inexplicable sense that the more he said he needed me, and the closer I came to him, the more he pulled away.

'Where are you going?' I'd called out one afternoon from the shed when he'd given up on a painting that wasn't working, and I saw him getting into his car.

'Fuck, Frances, what am I? A prisoner here? I'm moving my car out of the sun, is that all right?'

For the six months Clem and I had been in Bald Hill, all I'd seen was our storybook cottage, our work and our paintings, and our wrought-iron bed. The cold blue mornings and the colder nights, when our bodies would wrap together in sleep. The disappearing sunsets tinged with pink and gold. The mountains and the river and the endless enveloping sky.

I'd ignored my growing doubts and frustrations, and the unwelcome feeling that crept up on me when I was alone that something between us was terribly wrong, wanting to believe we were both in love with it all, in love with each other. But, the whole time, I now began to realise, one of us had been growing restless for it all to end.

I turned the handle and eased open the front door. Moonlight crashed into the cottage like a soundless wave. I stepped out onto the verandah and looked up at the sky, liquid black but awash with stars. Seemingly infinite. I felt so small below it.

I took Clem's leather jacket from the armchair by the door where he'd left it – one of the few things he hadn't packed yet – and slipped my arms inside it, my hands getting lost in the long sleeves.

I crossed the yard.

I had been painting at the river.

I had taken my fold-up easel and walked alone down the Candle River Track first thing in the morning, since the day had promised to be sunny and clear. I could hear the currawongs in the gums above me, their loud excited calls colliding, and the slow breathiness of the breeze. I was wearing denim shorts and a hat and sandals, and one of Clem's button-down shirts, which I had tied at the front to make it fit. I loved wearing his clothes. The way they fell generously around my body and carried his thick smoky smell.

I hadn't slept well the night before. Something kept waking me; a strange pinching and clenching in my gut, like a screw being twisted into my flesh. I wondered if it was just sadness manifesting as an ache in my body, since this would be our final week in Bald Hill, and I had no idea what was going to happen next.

Clem and I hadn't talked about it – our future – not once. Would I return to my room in the suburbs, to the stupor of my mother's flat? Could I even tolerate that now? Or did Clem have something else in mind, a plan to keep us together? I could live with him in his studio, I thought to myself as I walked along the narrow sloping track, red dirt and tiny rocks collecting inside my sandals, under my toes. I had no real belongings besides a handful of clothes and my satchel of art materials; I wouldn't take up a lot of space. I'd pay him rent, of course. Or work officially as his assistant in exchange. I didn't expect anything for nothing. I was a working artist now; I'd signed my contract with Tobias and was starting the paintings for my debut show.

I hadn't bothered to wake Clem to ask him to come with me down to the river. The last time I'd taken him there he hadn't enjoyed it at all, and neither had I.

'A river's a river,' he'd said on the sweltering uphill walk home, staying a metre ahead of me the whole time. 'I don't need to see it again.'

I'd made a frittata from one of the faded Italian cookbooks I'd found on a shelf in the kitchen, and packed it, still warm in the iron skillet, into a wicker basket for a picnic on the grassy bank. Then I'd grabbed a bottle of wine and a blanket I'd found in a squeaky old meat safe repurposed as a linen closet. The blanket was musty but lovely – blue and green plaid (Euan's taste, I'd guessed) – and large enough for the two of us to lie on.

But when Clem and I arrived at the river, already sweating from our walk down the track, it was impossible to find any shade. The sun was blasting from every angle, and there were few spots it couldn't reach. Even the trees offered little protection, the sun firing between their parched branches, boiling the ground so we couldn't stand on it in our bare feet.

I suggested a swim in the river to cool ourselves down before we ate, and started to undress. There was no one around – there was never anyone around, which was why I often went for a swim after I'd finished painting, lying on my back and letting my body just float, caressed by the weight of the water, my clothes, if I was wearing them, ballooning and turning translucent around me.

I was impatient now to feel the river's bracing coolness on my skin. The green surface was rippling, ever so gently and unhurriedly, whispering of the secret life that lay in its muddy depths. An ancient-looking iceberg-shaped rock jutted up from its middle, wide enough and tall enough, I'd found, to climb up and jump off.

I piled my clothes and sandals on the blanket and stood against the sun, naked. Sitting for Clem had made me less frightened of my body, or perhaps just more familiar with it. I knew the parts he liked, the areas where his eyes lingered while he painted me – my collarbone and my neck, the small taut rounds of my breasts, the dark sweep of wiry hair between my legs. I had noticed these parts too, in the round bathroom mirror I'd taken down off its hook and used when I'd tried to make some self-portraits back at the cottage.

It felt curious to be both painter and sitter, artist and subject, observer and object. I wasn't sure I liked it, having no distance between myself and the work; being so aware of myself, while at the same time trying not to be aware of myself at all. I did enjoy breaking my figure down into shapes, though, working out where the light hit my skin and where the dark patches sat. Where to inject colour and where to leave the canvas blank. Where to strip away unnecessary detail just as I would with a landscape.

I'd tried many times to paint Clem too, but he was so fidgety and distractible it never worked. After only a few minutes he would get up to make coffee or start cooking a meal, or put some music on the CD player, or walk out onto the verandah for a cigarette, and I could never finish what I'd started.

I found it was better to sketch him while he was asleep or hungover – the only times when he would stay still. I used ink to draw him lying in different positions on the bed or the lumpy couch. Often with one arm tucked behind his head, his thumb curled inside his fingers, his dark hair flopping over his eyes and cheek, a sharp elbow poking out, his knobbly feet crossed one over the other, his second toe longer than his big one. I'd used the ink sketches to help me paint a few portraits of him that way, but I wasn't happy with any of them. They all looked feeble and flat, and I wondered if I was just no good at painting figures or if there was something particular about Clem's body and face I didn't understand.

'You coming in?' I asked, holding out my hand.

'No, thanks. There could be anything in that river.'

He lay down on the blanket and covered his face with his straw hat that I noticed was losing its shape, and starting to fray at the crown.

'But you'll get too hot here, you'll burn.'

'So don't be too long.'

I hesitated. I'd imagined us swimming in the river together. Our bare bodies wading in, cautiously at first, then Clem plunging ahead of me into the cool water, and me diving in to follow him, my arms and legs pushing me deeper and deeper down to the churning river floor, my eyes wide open but seeing only murky greens and blackish browns. Then feeling a hand – Clem's – grip me calmly, protectively, like it had the first time we'd met, pulling me up for air, breaking me through the water's surface. The two of us clinging to each other in the middle of the river, threads of sunlight weaving through the trees, our bodies entwined, unassailable, our heads bent together, a silent circle of ripples surrounding us, slowly widening and lengthening, radiating out like the rings of a tree trunk, all the way to the river's edge.

'The water looks okay to me,' I said. 'It's usually pretty clean.'

Clem didn't reply. Most of his face was hidden under his hat.

'You don't have to go right in. Just come and dunk your feet.'

He pulled off his hat and glared at me. His hair and the skin around his temples were greasy with sweat.

'Do we have to do every little fucking thing together? Swim if you want to, or don't. I don't care.'

Clem covered his face with his hat again. For a moment I think I forgot to breathe, sickened to realise I was maddening him. I crossed my arms over my chest. I wished I hadn't been so quick to remove all my clothes.

'You don't like it here, do you?' I said softly.

'What's to like? There's nothing here. This place is a shithole.' Clem's hat wobbled on his face as he talked. I watched him lift a hand to hold it so it wouldn't tip off. 'Not your best idea. But it won't be a complete waste if we get some good paintings out of it.'

I should have heard then in his voice, in his words, in his reluctance to do anything with me at all besides fuck me and paint me in disembodied pieces, that Clem was already counting down the days until he could leave – both Bald Hill and me.

It was so clear to me now, as I stood at my fold-out easel with a paintbrush in hand, in my favourite spot near the rocky shallows where the ground was flat and the grey hollowed-out trunk of a she-oak lay like a defeated and decomposing beast, that I had served my purpose for Clem and become something peripheral to be discarded. In the months we'd lived at Bald Hill he'd made twelve new paintings for his show in Melbourne that he'd told me he was proud of, all of which I'd helped to create – stretching and priming the canvases, painting in the backgrounds, working on the details he didn't have time or patience for; and all of them of me, though nowhere was I recognisable, my body digested and regurgitated as a pair of legs, a set of arms with no hands, a bit of breast, all aimlessly careering like space junk in a blue-black void.

I felt dizzy, as if I were unspooling. I had to sit down on the tree trunk. Had to drop my head between my legs, as if it were an anchor that might steady me, and catch my breath.

My arms were trembling. My head was spinning. My stomach was still aching. Twisting. Screwing. I thought I might be sick. And now my breasts ached too.

=

Clem's Mercedes was parked in the narrow dirt lane up behind the cottage. Even in the middle of the night the car seemed to glow, moonlight bouncing off its silver hub caps and round headlights. As I walked towards it, my calves sensing the sharp rise in the ground it was far too dark to see, I pictured Clem driving it out of town first thing in the morning, its wheels carelessly tossing up dust, its sleek body incongruous with the rugged landscape disappearing behind it; the passenger seat empty, or perhaps loaded with his suitcases – either way, no sign that I had ever been there. The longer I stared at it, the more the car appeared to me as some sort of menacing creature lying in wait in the dark. It seemed to be mocking me with all I was about to lose. Tomorrow it would drive Clem out of my life; I was done with.

I pulled Clem's jacket tighter to my chest as I kept on walking. My breath showed like smoke in the blue night air. The dirt below my feet was cold and uneven, and as I entered the lane I felt a rock – or was it a stick? – stab my left heel, as though the earth itself were cautioning me to go no further. Without thinking, I picked it up and threw it straight at the car. I heard it hit – a brief sound swallowed quickly by the air – and hoped it left a dent. I felt pathetic. I didn't know what I was doing, or why I was wandering half naked in the dark at two am. I only knew I had not been able to sleep, or to ignore a compulsion to see for myself everything Clem had packed into his car. Maybe then I would believe that what was happening was real.

'I won a residency,' he'd announced, his dark eyes shining as he pulled his CDs off the bookshelf and loaded them into a cardboard box. There was a corkscrew and a bottle of red wine on the side table by the sofa, and beside them a single glass.

I had just walked back from the river, and was standing in the front doorway holding my fold-up easel. I had oil paint on my face or in my hair; now that I was inside I could smell it – the pernicious tang of paint close by. A patch of skin on the back of my neck was tingling with sunburn.

'You never said you were applying for a residency.' I put my easel down on the floor. Through the doorway to the bedroom I could see Clem's suitcase, open like a laughing mouth on our bed.

'I only did it at the last minute,' he said, closing the cardboard box. 'Never expected to win.'

He picked up a roll of masking tape and as he pulled a long strip off, it screeched. He bit the strip from the roll and stuck it down to close the box.

'Where's it to?' I heard myself ask.

'Barcelona. For six months.'

He wouldn't look at me. Just kept ripping and sticking the tape, the sound of it excruciating.

'When do you leave?'

'Four weeks. But I should head out of here tomorrow. Start getting organised. Find a tenant for the studio, sort out my passport – I don't even know if it's up to date.'

He ran his hand across the lid of the box and tapped it, satisfied it was sealed.

'But we still have a few more days,' I said. 'Or longer if we want. The landlord doesn't need us to leave. We don't have to rush off anywhere.' I wasn't sure what I was saying anymore. I could hear the ugly desperation in my voice, the panic rising like the quickest of tides to overwhelm me, but I couldn't help it, couldn't stop. 'And if you've still got four weeks . . .'

Clem looked at me. He smiled.

'We've had a good time, Frances. Haven't we?'

He was ending it. He was leaving. Or, more precisely, he was leaving me. In four weeks he would be flying halfway across the world to Barcelona, probably on his way to a studio apartment overlooking narrow medieval streets. He would find another model there, I had no doubt. Someone beautiful and Spanish. Someone new to fill the six months.

'You've loved it here, I know you have,' he said, walking to the kitchen to get another glass from the shelf beside the cooker. 'And you've come such a long way, I've seen that. It's been great for your work. Brilliant. But not mine.' He walked back, and put the second glass down on the side table next to his own. Then he picked up the bottle of wine and the corkscrew, and began twisting it into the cork. 'This place doesn't talk to me at all. I really thought it would. It's talked to so many artists. But for me it's just too . . .' He paused and squinted as he searched for the right word. 'Boring,' he said finally, removing the cork.

I would never know if he chose that word intentionally. If he considered the way it might echo, or intended for it to shatter me in the way that it did. Probably not, I think.

He poured the red wine into both glasses, filling them to the top.

'But you've made so many paintings here,' I said. 'At least twelve that are strong enough to show, you said so.'

'Sure,' he nodded. 'But I can paint figures anywhere. Doesn't have to be here.'

'What about your show in Melbourne? I thought it was so important.'

'The show's done. It's all finished, ready to go. I'll miss my opening, but there are worse things. Don't think I'll be worrying about it from Barcelona.'

He picked up both glasses and handed me one.

'But thank you, Frances. I mean it. The paintings of you are unbelievable. They're going to sell like crazy, I know it. And get me a cracking review.'

I looked at the cottage. So sunny and pretty. That rosy afternoon light swimming in through the windows, spilling over the room, bleaching everything, blurring the edges of shapes.

I thought of Freya. 'He'll tire of you,' she had said at the strange dinner at Lydia and Theo's. 'He always does.'

I had thought she was trying to belittle me or put me in my place; eject me as if I were a splinter that had snuck beneath Clem's skin. But Freya had been trying to warn me, I saw now. She knew Clem better than I did and had probably seen this situation play out before. I had been a willing and obedient model. A pliant and guileless lover. A passive, infatuated, unsophisticated girl prepared to do anything to keep him close. But those qualities were not special or irreplaceable, they could be found anywhere. It struck me that what in particular had condemned me – what must have seemed romantic and attractive to Clem at the start but was now unacceptable to him, maybe even intolerable – was my being an artist too, potentially even a good one.

'Cheers,' Clem said, touching his glass to mine.

'To what?'

'Us,' he said, as he slid his fingers under the collar of my shirt – his shirt – and pushed it aside to kiss my collarbone.

'It doesn't have to end badly, does it? We can be grown-ups.' His lips inched up my neck, their soft dampness and familiarity soothing my burned skin.

'No,' I agreed, his breath in my ear, his hand moving slowly over my breast. 'It doesn't have to end badly.'

I found the matches in the pocket of Clem's leather jacket. A crumpled box of Redheads he'd bought from the general store (it still had the sticky yellow price tag) and forgotten about. There were hardly any matches left inside it, and most of those remaining were snapped in half.

I've often wondered what might have been different if I hadn't felt it there, keeping company with a dirty twenty-cent coin and a safety pin. If I hadn't picked his jacket up off the chair in the first place, hadn't seen it there. If I'd stayed in bed beside him, pretending to sleep, and simply waved him goodbye in the morning. If I hadn't walked outside and stared for so long at his car that I'd started to see it as something alive, as some sort of foe. If the driver-side door hadn't been unlocked and I hadn't opened it and sat in the front seat, my bare legs pale and covered in goosebumps, my hands shaking, my fingers hunting the glove box for something sharp with which to gouge the dashboard or rip open the leather seats. If I hadn't screamed with rage at the unfeeling dark when

I couldn't find anything but cassette tapes and rubbish. If I hadn't leaned back on the seat, tired and defeated, and remembered my first time in the car, on that steamiest of days, seeing Bald Hill out the passenger window in my pink dress. If I hadn't buried my hands in the pockets of Clem's jacket to get them warm, my eyes sore and swollen from lack of sleep, from staring so long down the hill at the cottage where I knew he was sleeping, soundly and unaffected. If I'd understood my breasts ached for a reason, that there was something forming inside me that needed to be protected; then the idea might never have occurred to me.

But on that night, looking in the rear-view mirror at the stack of Clem's paintings on the back seat, and knowing I would find more in the boot – paintings of me, parts of me, a slaughterhouse of me – it was all I could think of and all I could see. The only thing that made sense.

And I could smell them. Clem's paintings. Below the membrane, one or two were still fresh, still wet.

There was a cardboard box on the passenger seat beside me. While I'd been down at the river, Clem must have packed all his paints and brushes into it, and all his other tools and materials from the shed. The plastic bottle of turps was lying at the top, jutting out of the box, nosing open the lid.

I don't remember picking it up or twisting the cap. I don't even remember getting out of the car and opening the boot, but obviously I did. I've tried so hard to recall if I used the whole bottle or if I only tipped out a little. But it makes no difference, I guess. Turps is so combustible it wouldn't have taken much.

What I remember clearly are the matches. And the frustration I felt when the first one didn't catch. When the cold blue dark snuffed it out as it flew from my hand to the car and I whispered, 'Fuck!' and realised I would have to step closer for it to light.

I let the second match burn longer, holding it between my fingers until the heat began to sting, and then I threw it into the boot.

For months afterwards – years, really, if I'm honest, and sometimes even now if I let myself get too run down – the image would return to me in the dark or in the milky dawn as I sat half-awake breastfeeding, repeating and repeating like a film scene on a loop, never the possibility of a different ending. The lit match lands on the stack of paintings. The top canvas flares, a perfect rectangle of fire. The flame roars and expands, developing arms and legs like a fiendish octopus that swims up out of the boot, twists in the air, and dives down into the back seat, licking everything in its path with its feverish red tongue. One of the side windows pops, then another one, the sounds like gunshots. The car is hissing and spitting, convulsing, spewing orange and red, tails of fire and thick smoke swirling up to a wide black sky littered with stars.

Down the hill, in the cottage, the bedroom light flicks on. The window floods with yellow.

FIVE

Gold-panning (and C's pink line), oil on linen, 50 × 60 cm

I don't notice the email from Clementine until I stop for lunch. Checking my watch, though, I see it is closer to dinnertime. The rain outside the studio has ebbed without my noticing and the drizzly sky has darkened to a moonish grey. I've been painting for seven hours straight, struggling with a landscape – an eroded gold mine down a gully off the Candle River Track. I'm exhausted, and glad to have an excuse to step away from it for a while. I remember the egg sandwich I packed for myself this morning and unwrap it as I click open the email, willing my internet connection, always erratic at the studio, to stay stable.

bonjour maman,

see? my french is improving! no more disasters . . . i hope! i was so stressed about all that salmon that i invited everyone from my floor over to share it with me and we put it on baguettes. tres french! we had to eat it sitting on the floor because they only give you one desk and two chairs here in each artist's studio. but everyone thought it was hilarious i'd mixed up four and fourteen when i asked the fish guy at the market for pieces of salmon. ingo who's a filmmaker on scholarship here too but from germany said i should have just told him i'd made a mistake. er . . . ingo doesn't know how atrocious my french is. hey, i heard from dad this morning. he rang the main phone downstairs instead of using the code i gave him for my room, and madame brunel had to run up five flights of stairs to get me, which definitely pissed her off. but they forgive you anything here if you're australian. it's like you've come from the end of the earth so they go easy on you. it'd blow their minds if i told them i grew up in a house made of mud and sticks. anyway, are you going to dad's opening? it sounds HUUUUGE. he's sending me a catalogue but i really wish i could be there to see it. and the gallery's doing all this merch like t-shirts and jigsaw puzzles and mugs with his paintings on them, so i made him promise to send me a package with one of everything. i think he was really calling to find out if you'd be there. he asked a few

times if you were going and i said i didn't know. he thought maybe you hadn't got the invite because you haven't rsvp'd. but you got it right? he's nervous because there's that painting of you in it. the one in the pink dress. he doesn't want you to freak out if you get there and see it printed on a massive banner out the front of the gallery. (haha just kidding. there's no way he'd do that . . . is there?????) maybe rsvp so he knows. i told him he should just call you himself but you know what he's like.
love you,
c x

I read the email three times, imagining her there, my grown-up girl in her own studio at the Cité des arts in the Marais, overlooking Pont Marie and the Seine. I imagine her impromptu dinners on the floor and her exciting new friends and her funny mishaps at the market. There seems little left now of the baby girl with the warm milk smell who I took to the river and panned for gold with, her chubby little hands swirling a shallow pan in the muddy water, her worm-like fingers picking out the rocks and giving them names before plonking them, one by one, back in the river.

'The gold's the heaviest than everything else,' she would inform me with authority, forgetting that I had been the one to tell her. 'It keeps in the pan when all the dirt washes gone.'

She was so much like Clem. She'd inherited his warm olive skin, his curly dark hair and hooded eyes, his innate ease and openness with people. For me, there had been no question she should also inherit his first name.

And whenever they saw each other – only a little at first, but more and more as she grew older and wanted to know him, wanted to see the world beyond Bald Hill – the two of them got along so naturally. As though she'd been born knowing the tricky way to Clem's heart.

Or perhaps, I think now, she had been the one to open it. A loud little girl bursting into a gloomy terrace, throwing open all the windows and doors, letting in the light.

Having her did not murder my practice, as Albert had darkly warned. Interrupted it, certainly. Sent things wildly askew. And without the support of Euan and Matteo, who gave me the cottage rent-free for as long as I needed, and even came to stay with me for the first few months after she was born, I could not have managed. They would rock her to sleep when I could no longer keep my eyes open, deal with the endless washing, cook me the most beautiful hearty meals. (Turning to my mother was not something I once thought of. And would have been pointless anyway. If I had asked her, she would not have come. And I would not have wanted her there.)

'We've both been dying for an excuse to take some time off and come back here to Bald Hill,' Euan had reassured me late one night in the kitchen while making us a pot of tea, after Clementine had finally stopped crying and I'd told him it was expecting too much of him and Matteo to continue helping me in this way. 'We've never known the pleasure of a baby in our world,' Euan had said. 'She's got a voice on her, that's for sure. But she's such a delight, I'm afraid we've both gone a bit gaga.' He squeezed my wrist, mischievously. 'Wait till you see all the jewellery I have in mind for her. Oh boy.'

But she had enriched my work too. Expanded it. Brought a new efficiency, a spontaneity, to my paintings. Added a depth and a quality of feeling that weren't there before. Made it grander. More immediate and more fluid. Widened my vision and even helped me see the landscape afresh.

When she had grown enough to fit in a papoose I would carry her with me down to the river or up to one of the lookouts, and when we got there she would lie on a blanket on the grass beside me, staring up at the sky and the tall eucalypts festooned with leaves, her hooded aquamarine eyes shifting to catch each call from a bird, each flap of a wing, while I painted.

And when she was bigger but still too small to walk on her own, I would hold her on my hip, her bottom pressed to my side, her round little face peering outwards, while I made paintings at my easel in the shed, one of my arms hooked around her middle, the other directing a brush.

Once, when I had nearly finished a painting I intended to hang in my second solo show with Tobias (the first had shocked me by being a sellout, allowing me to pay back Euan and Matteo some of the rent I owed – not that they'd ever asked – and buy myself a car), Clementine flung out her hand and stuck her fingers into the canvas, smearing them into the paint, swiping them from one side of the work to the other.

I took a step back and, tired and frustrated, looked to see what she had done: added her own blatant mark to the picture; an unexpected bald line of bubblegum pink.

In the end I left it there. It lifted the whole painting. Made it sing.

A couple of months before her first birthday, without any warning, Albert came to visit. He'd driven to Bald Hill alone and had booked himself a room overnight at the pub. He brought two gifts: a little wooden box of half-sticks of pastels from La Maison du Pastel in Paris – the store that had made pastels for Degas, he seemed to enjoy telling me – and an unframed painting, one of his empty interiors he must have known I loved.

GIRL IN A PINK DRESS

Neither of us brought up Clem, or his exhibition the previous year in Melbourne. How I'd left him with no paintings to hang in the show and no time to produce any more. How he'd had to scrape together whatever finished works he could find in his studio – and how most of those, as it turned out, were of me.

He'd exhibited the *Girl in a pink dress* painting, along with eight other 'straight' portraits he'd made of me during our first blissful months together, before we'd gone to Bald Hill. The critics had, unexpectedly, gone wild. They'd applauded 'the bold and luxurious injection of colour' in Clem's work, and the 'new maturity and seriousness of his approach'. Even the previously scathing art critic from the newspaper had dubbed *Girl in a pink dress* Clem's 'breakthrough painting'.

The show was sold out before it even opened. Clem's Melbourne dealer had invited her dearest and most important collectors to the gallery for a private preview on the afternoon she'd hung the show, two days before its official opening, and every painting was sold within the first ten minutes. While numerous offers were made on it, *Girl in a pink dress* was marked 'NFS' – not for sale.

'Have you been doing any painting?' Albert asked.

'Of course. Whenever I can.'

We were sitting together at the kitchen table. I'd made him an espresso from the silver coffee pot Matteo had left me and shown me how to use, and I'd opened a packet of biscuits I'd found in the cupboard, though neither of us had picked one up. Clementine was sitting on my lap, babbling and wriggling, chewing noisily on a piece of banana she was gripping between her sticky hands.

'She's not following much of a routine right now. Or as soon as she starts to, she changes it the next day. I think she's got more teeth coming.' I wiped away the soggy chunk of banana that had slipped from Clementine's mouth onto my shirt. 'It's a bit all over the place. But she's mostly sleeping through now, so nights are good for work.'

Albert nodded. I saw him look around the kitchen. I hadn't washed the dishes from the day before – they were still stacked in the sink – or tidied the wooden table we were sitting at. On it were baby clothes and wooden toys and pieces of paperwork and a cold, forgotten cup of tea, all of which I had pushed to one end when he'd arrived.

For no apparent reason Clementine made a sharp noise and writhed unhappily, throwing what was left of her banana at the floor. It landed on the side of Albert's trouser leg, then dropped down onto his shoe. He looked at me, as if waiting for instruction on how the situation should be dealt with.

'Sorry, she gets cranky when she's tired. I might put her down for a sleep. If you don't mind waiting?'

'Not at all.'

'Here, use this.' I handed him a sponge to clean his trousers and shoe.

I could see Albert thought I was done for. That I had squandered all my talent and promise for nothing but a sinking domesticity. That he viewed this as a loss, an unfortunate waste; but, more than that, that he feared it was dangerous for me.

He had his reasons for thinking this way, I knew. The memory of Eva and what she had done was never far from him, even then. He had never stopped loving her, that was clear to me. Or escaped from the grief of her devastating decision; it lived with him always, was part of him. But there must have been more to Eva's act, I'd always felt, than Albert's reading of it. And at times I caught myself wondering if he had ever considered what role he might have played, large or small, in her desperate unhappiness. The only thing I could be sure of was that there had been much more to Eva than Albert or I, or perhaps anyone, would ever know; even Clem, who had always seemed to me so hesitant, even detached, whenever he'd spoken of her, which was not often. I could never quite tell if he loved Eva or hated her. Probably both.

'Would you like to see the studio?' I said once I'd settled Clementine down for a nap in her cot and returned to Albert in the kitchen. 'Have a look at what I'm working on, tell me what you think.'

'Please, show me,' Albert said, eagerly standing up. I saw that while I'd been gone he had tucked a note behind his painting telling me, as I later read, to sell it should I ever need the money. I realised this was his restrained way of offering care and protection, of showing love – his paintings were all he knew to give, and I always appreciated the one he gave me, and hung it proudly on my wall.

I led the way around the back of the cottage to the shed, Albert walking slowly behind me. When we were almost there, sensing he had stopped, I turned around to see what had happened. He was standing by the quince tree, staring out at the mountains that wrapped like arms around the desiccated township, a rust-coloured autumn sky quivering above it, warm and translucent, tissue-thin.

Maybe to me, or maybe only to himself, Albert said softly, 'Try painting that.'

The following year, after the resounding success of his commercial show in Melbourne, Clem entered *Girl in a pink dress* in the Baines Award, the country's newest and most lucrative prize for portraiture, which offered double the money and twice the street cred of the Archibald Prize. The day of the announcement, according to Tobias (who had an ear to everyone in the art world, it seemed), a buyer from Sydney, an owner of luxury hotels, offered

GIRL IN A PINK DRESS

Clem two hundred and fifty thousand dollars for *Girl in a pink dress*. And though it was more money than he'd ever been paid for a painting to date, Clem politely refused. The following day a second buyer doubled the offer and was met with the same answer.

A couple of months later, after the frenzied publicity of the prize had died down, and Clem was no longer on the news or on the covers of the papers, a third buyer made him an offer, and he finally relented, selling the painting for an undisclosed sum.

I put in a few more hours on the painting. I scrape away a section of background that isn't working and try to build it back up again, remake it afresh. But it keeps resisting. There are too many layers now. Too many wayward marks I keep having to wipe off with a rag. It feels as if none of my brushstrokes have any intention or purpose, as if I'm pushing paint around the canvas simply to fill up space.

I put down my brush.

I go to my desk and open the drawer that's missing one of its wooden knobs. The envelope is still there, among my other mail, the flap torn open from when it arrived nearly a month ago.

I pick it up. Slide out the glossy official invitation from the Art Gallery of New South Wales to *Clem Hughes:*

Painting's Heir. A celebration of works created by the artist over the past two and a half decades from public, corporate and private collections from around Australia and the world.

One of Clem's faceless black and white heads stares back at me from the invitation. I recognise it from that first show I ever saw of his at Porter Street Gallery. For some reason now the image, with its empty and unseeing eyes, its impenetrable blankness, reminds me of my mother, who I sometimes call or, if I've been in Sydney for work, visit at her flat on my drive home.

I was always so afraid of ending up just like her. Her remote sleepwalking stare. Her plastic bags of takeaway and her television. Her bedroom door always closed.

But when I think of my first room – of how everything in it was canary yellow, and of the hopes she must have had when she'd decorated it that way – I wonder if perhaps it was not my mother who gave up on me, who ignored me, who didn't care if I existed or not. That it might have been the other way around, that I gave up on her. She never loved me very well, it's true, but she never left me.

I turn the invite over, already knowing what I will find.

Clem's handwriting. The black ink of a fountain pen pressed deep into the thick paper. Still so blithely confident.

I run my finger over the letters. They are not much. Five words. But they are something. They are what's left in the pan after twenty-five years.

Hope you can come.
Clem

I see him running up the hill from the cottage in the dark. He has no clothes on, no shoes. The ground is slippery with dew and he stumbles, his legs tripping over themselves as if he has woken from a malicious spell to find them boneless. It's the first time his body has ever looked incompetent.

I am sitting on the ground, wrapped in his jacket, watching the car and the paintings burn.

He is yelling at me, his face red and monstrous in the firelight, his bare feet kicking at the ground. He is like an animal, turning his face up to the stars, the moon, and howling. He is clutching me, shaking me by the shoulders, trying to haul me up, but I am like a rubber doll. I can't stand, can't make out what he is saying. His lips are moving frantically but there's no sound. It's as though he is underwater, sinking further and further away into the deep. And all I can hear are the shrieks of the fire as it devours the car.

=

It's what I think of now as I stand in the gallery, surrounded by fifty or so works spanning the past quarter century of Clem's impressive career. The old men in grey suits who recognised me a moment ago have moved on to the next room of paintings, where Clem's second wife, Valentina, and their twin toddler boys are waiting. I think of saying hello, introducing myself, since we haven't officially met. But she hasn't seen me and has her hands full with the two squirming boys. I let the moment pass.

Clem is a few metres away, talking to a journalist covering the show. Albert is beside him in a smart houndstooth jacket, leaning on a walking stick.

'I'd say it's the opposite, if anything,' I hear Clem say. 'The older I get, the less I feel I know about painting, the more I have to look at—'

His eyes catch mine and for a second he loses his track. I am relieved when he smiles.

'Look, the boy still hasn't figured out yet,' Albert tells the journalist, his voice laboured and shaky now, each word an effort for him, 'if painting is more about lying or revealing a truth. Most of these pictures here,' he says, lifting his walking stick and waving it around the room, 'are probably lies.'

I look back at myself in the pink dress for what will likely be the last time. This painting is owned by a private collector in Singapore, on loan to the gallery for the duration of the exhibition. After that it will be packed into a wooden crate, loaded onto a truck, then a plane, and returned to its home on a wall I'll never see.

I feel a strange sense of ownership over it. A desire to hold on to it. To pull it off the wall and take it home with me. But to keep it, or keep it hidden, I am not sure. I feel a perplexing mix of pride and humiliation to see myself young and giant on the wall in my pink dress.

But it's only now, as I offer her my silent goodbye, that I realise the woman in the painting is not me. She wears my dress. She has my body and my face. But she is a story, an argument, a warning.

She is a self-portrait of the artist as his long-ago love.

She is a boy in a gloomy terrace, sitting in silence while his father draws.

She is Eva under the water, her corpse swirling with the catfish and the eels.

EPILOGUE

Study for self-portrait, pencil on paper, 77 × 57 cm

My high beams paint the night ink-blue as I steer my ute up the steep mountain. The skulking fog becomes more brazen the higher I drive. Not that it matters. I could probably find my way home with my eyes closed. I've lost count of how many times I've driven up and down this track. I know every turn and dog-leg by heart.

But it's here, as my tyres crunch loose gravel as I pick up speed, and the radio falters and crackles with static as I nose out of the bend like it always does, that I feel something massive hit the front of the ute. The great weight thumps the bonnet and jerks the ute sideways like a pinball. I throw my foot to the brake and grip the steering wheel, wrestling to control the vehicle as it skids in the gravel, its rear sliding with a mind of its own, lurching downwards, off the road, until I feel it suddenly stop.

My headlights are shining at a huddle of skinny trees.

I open the door and step out. I feel the fog, cold and accusing on my skin. I run my hand across the bonnet. There is a deep dent, maybe a metre wide, as if something has taken a bite out of it. I turn and look behind me. A long low shape lies in the middle of the road. It is cloaked in fog but I can see part of it moving.

I take my torch from the glove box and begin to walk slowly towards it, a line of shadowy light stretching ahead of me. With each step I feel more and more as if I am drowning. As if the fog is turning to water and burying me whole.

The roo is shattered but she is not dead, so I keep my distance. Her skull is bleeding and her tail is half-severed, but her back legs are thrashing in the torchlight like fish in a bucket. I see no lump or movement in her pouch. I search her eyes but her gaze is elsewhere.

I get back in the ute and try the engine. It coughs but doesn't sound too badly damaged. Fixing my eyes on the rear-view mirror, I manoeuvre the ute so it's in line with the roo's head. I put the gear in reverse, my foot to the pedal, and accelerate.

=

I drive into town. Past the rows of maples that have no leaves left to drop. Past the pub whose lights are out. Past the patch of ground where I once saw a girl etch her name into the frost.

I turn left and then quickly right, approaching my cottage from the back lane, as is my habit. The house will be cold but I'm too exhausted to find kindling and light the fire. I'll plug in the oil heater instead. I'll fill the bath and get clean. I'll eat something.

'Hit a roo, did ya?' says a thin scratchy voice in the dark.

'Yeah,' I say, turning off the engine and stepping out of the ute.

'Bugger,' my neighbour Rina says.

She's wearing loose jeans that swish around her scrawny legs as she walks towards me, and a shaggy poncho with sparkly tassels that make her look like an emu, proud of her plumage. Even in the pitch dark, I know her eyelids will be drooping at the corners from too many beers; I can smell them on her, thick and fermented. She must have finished work at the pub and walked the long way home.

'Big one, eh?' Rina says, looking the dead roo over as it lies motionless in the tray.

'Came out of nowhere.'

'Musta shocked the shit outta ya.'

I nod.

'How'd you get her in here? She's a beast.'

'I don't know,' I say.

'Can't have done it yerself?'

I feel Rina stare at me. Take in the smears of blood on my shirt, my hands, my face.

Then she laughs, pointing at the big dent.

'Fucked your car up,' she says.

I nod and begin to walk down the cobbled path to my back door. There's a shy yellow glow coming from the kitchen window, and I feel glad I left a light on inside.

'What're ya gonna do with her?' Rina calls out, rubbing her hands up and down her arms to keep warm. 'She'll stink like shit in the morning.'

I look up into the dark and think of the roo's heavy, unwieldy body in my arms. Contorted and crushed but still muscular, still proud.

'I'm going to paint her,' I say.

I can see it already – the painting. A self-portrait in my studio. I am standing beside my easel in my painting clothes, a brush in one hand and a dirty rag in the other. The mangled roo is lying at my bare feet, stiff and unblinking.